shakespearecore

Five Shakespeare-inspired Stories

carly stevens

Copyright © 2026 by Carly Stevens

All rights reserved.

No part of this book may be reproduced in any form or by any electronic or mechanical means, including information storage and retrieval systems, without written permission from the author, except for the use of brief quotations in a book review.

Without in any way limiting the author's [and publisher's] exclusive rights under copyright, any use of this publication to "train" generative artificial intelligence (AI) technologies to generate text is expressly prohibited.

Email carly@carly-stevens.com with questions or to request permission to use portions of the text.

contents

Preface	5
1. Camp Oberon *90's summer camp (A Midsummer Night's Dream)*	9
2. Transcript of Police Interview [Horatio Flite] *Southern Crime (Hamlet)*	43
3. What You Will *Winter Cottagecore (Twelfth Night)*	55
4. To Have Had So Much Blood *Gothic Horror (Macbeth)*	71
5. For Anne Hathaway *Elegiac poetry*	103
6. Christmas in Paris *Vintage Christmas (Hamlet)*	107
Also by Carly Stevens	117
About the Author	119

preface

I first read Shakespeare when I was twelve, and it's hooked me ever since.

No, I haven't read his entire catalogue.

Yes, I'm obsessed with *Hamlet* to the point of writing an entire novel from Laertes' point of view.

One of the great strengths of Shakespeare's work is that it covers to much of the human experience. He wrote good plays and bad plays, funny plays and sad plays, gory plays and fairy plays. And he was kind enough to leave room in the cracks between lines for us to find ourselves. His stories are like the old myths that can be re-formed in different ways.

Your first clue about my love of stories and words should have come with my declaration about loving Shakespeare when I was still in middle school. That love turned into a career as an indie author.

One of the tough things about being an indie author is that so many people tell you to stay in your lane. Create a series in a specific sub-genre and stay there until you build

Preface

an audience. Good advice, but that's tough for me to do. Then I had a brainstorm. What if I wrote in all the sparkly, dark, romantic, tragic, childish, or weird genres and put them under the same big umbrella (Shakespeare, in the case of this first -core collection)? That way, when I got the feral urge to write poetry or horror or a Christmas story, that writing could live somewhere.

My hope is that you enjoy this kaleidoscope of experiences and voices. Feel free to skip around to whatever you feel like reading. Writing *Shakespearecore* was a challenge and a chance to stretch my wings. I look forward to experimenting with even more styles and genres in the future.

Thank you for giving me that opportunity.

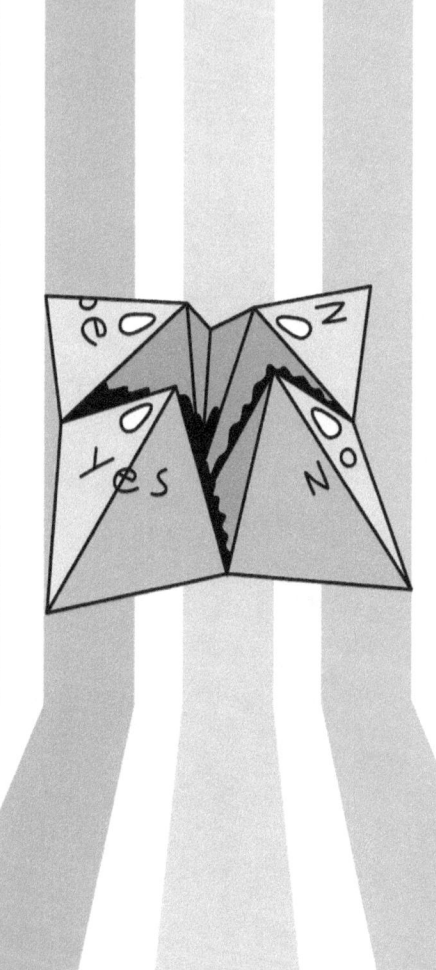

camp oberon

. . .

90's summer camp (A
Midsummer Night's Dream)

1

WHEN THE BUS passes the sign to Camp Oberon, I grab my pillow and sleeping bag closer with excitement. The air smells like dust and toffee, and I cannot wait to jump down the steps and run to my cabin. Hopefully, I get the same one as last year.

"Look!" my friend Helen cries, gripping my arm.

I squeal before I even see what she's looking at. Next to the dirt road, which is as blinding as white snow, counselors are setting up plastic tables with boxes of frozen Otter Pops on them. There are other thingies too, set out in baskets, but I can't see because of the blinding light and the moving bus. The camp has a general store where you can use real money or tickets you earn over your time at camp to buy prizes. Last year, I won a ton of tickets for winning a hula hoop competition, award for cleanest cabin, and four rounds of foosball.

We lumber forward, past the counselors who pause to wave at us.

I wave back enthusiastically. Last year, we got snap bracelets that said Camp Oberon on them. I kept mine on my dresser all year so I would remember to bring it. The first day is always toward the end of June. It's like the summer is halfway over before we finally get to see our friends at camp.

"Ooh!" I turn back to Helen. She looks right over my head to see out the window. She's like a skinny stick. Really pretty. Even her eyebrows are skinny and I'm so jealous. I'm super short, but she says I'm little and fierce. I like that. I'm totally fierce.

Another busload of campers rolls slowly to a stop ahead of us, and kids file out. They're all eleven or twelve, like Helen and me. Some of them look like little kids as they lug their heavy luggage over the rough terrain over the road and between the trees. Counselors are pointing them to the right cabins. Others look like grown-ups, like men and women.

My stomach constricts. Helen and I *have* to be in the same cabin together. And it has to be Quince, my favorite cabin. I have camp friends that I see every year, but Helen is my best friend forever. I'm literally wearing friendship bracelet next to the Camp Oberon snap bracelet that says "Helen." Hers says "Mia."

I blow out a breath. Nothing will keep us apart.

She points. "Is that Trey? And Xander?"

I crane to look. Two figures are stepping off the bus, backpacks slung carelessly over their shoulders. Xander's hair has grown out since the last time I saw him, and Trey is at least a few inches taller. I'd probably only come up to his chest. Both of them wear sweatbands on their wrists. Trey has on a white T-shirt with the Tasmanian Devil on it that makes his skin look extra dark. He almost looks like Michael Jordan in that Nike commercial. I've seen Trey play basketball and he is really good. Not Michael Jordan good. But I still love watching him play with Xander. He grins at his best friend and my heart does a funny somersault.

Last summer, five of us did everything together—the two of us girls, Trey, Xander, and Robbie—but now they look so cool… Would they still want to hang out with us? I didn't want them to treat me like a little kid.

My dad would just say to stay away from all boys, but he's just an overprotective parent. I managed to get him to say that Xander was maybe okay after I told him that Xander's dad had the same job as him, but I never got him to think Trey was cool.

"We should say hi," Helen insists as the bus finally creaks and hisses to a stop. Pale dust swirls up around the smudgy windows. I squeeze my pillow and sleeping bag tighter. They both have *Lion King* print on them. A second ago, I loved that, but now it seems like something a kid would like, and I'm going into middle school after this summer. I bite my lip.

"You okay, Mia?"

I snap my attention back to my friend. The boys won't think she's a little kid. Too bad I didn't grow much this year. "Yeah. Whatever."

I stand and struggle to pull my backpack from the storage above the seats. People press around me.

Robbie won't think I'm just a kid. He's the kind of guy who pulls pranks and plays a lot of games, but not in a kiddish way. Our whole group thought he was the most fun. I have no idea what school he goes to—it isn't Athenian Elementary or Amazon Middle.

As Helen stands to follow me out of the bus, I decide we're going to find Robbie first. *Then* we'll figure out where the boys are staying and go all together.

I squint into the white-bright sun as I step down the deep bus steps to the dirt road. Shouts and talking are everywhere. Friends hug each other. Counselors try to keep order, but everything is way too exciting. From the ground, I can see the lake through the trees and the top of the ropes course peeking through the pine forest.

I feel better already.

"All the girls on this bus will stay in the Woods Cabin," someone with a clipboard yells. "Bring all your luggage to the cabin and then come back here!"

I frown. Helen appears at my side.

"The Woods?" she repeats, drawing out the name.

"That's bogus!" I say. The Woods is the farthest cabin from the dining hall, the general store, and everything else. "Can't we stay in Quince? That's where we've been the last two years."

The lady looks up from her clipboard. "Nope. That cabin's already taken."

I grind my teeth.

"The Woods is right down that path at the end," she explains.

Helen pulls me forward to stop me from saying anything else. "It'll be fine," she whispers.

"But—"

"Did you see where Trey and Xander went?"

I shake my head. I lost track of them after I got off the

bus. "We'll probably see them at the Otter Pop station if we hurry."

We shuffle faster.

"Wait!" Helen exclaims, pulling a disposable camera out of the side pocket of her backpack. She backs up, aiming at me. I set my stuff in the dirt and fling my arms in the air, a big smile on my face. "Perfect!"

"Now you." I take the camera, roll the film forward, and snap a picture of Helen looking amazing as always. She cocks her head to the side with a coy look. The sunlight gleams on the layers of her hair and half-shadows the tattoo choker necklace she's wearing.

"That'll be a good one," I say, handing the camera back and awkwardly grabbing all my baggage. Who knew a few T-shirts and a toothbrush could be so heavy?

I can't wait to get rid of all this stuff and get back to the main area to look for the boys, including Robbie.

Now that we're getting close to the tree line, it smells nice, but I can't help thinking about what this place will be like after dark…

2

Even flashlights don't do much in the pitch blackness of the woods after nightfall, if I remember right. There was one night when I was only ten that Robbie told us the scariest story. We were all tired from a night of games and karaoke, so I felt like I couldn't move from the big campfire they'd set up. It's embarrassing, but I jumped a tiny bit when Robbie turned on a flashlight under his face, so it was lit from below. The shadows were terrifying. But then it got worse. His story gave me nightmares for a week.

Okay, not a week. Sometimes I still think I see the Puck out of the corner of my eye if the room is *really* dark.

The Puck is a creature that lives in the woods and can change shape. That means that any tree or bunny you pass could be the Puck and you wouldn't know it. Did your backpack just tip over and pour out all your folders? That's exactly the kind of thing the Puck likes to do. He can also make you see things that aren't there. Robbie said the Puck's favorite prey is sleeping campers because he can sneak up without them knowing. He can make something crash to the floor. Or, even worse, he can turn you into a creature like himself, doomed to stay in the forest for eternity.

I dart my eyes from side to side, but it's daytime. No way the Puck would be here now.

My breathing has gotten heavier by the time we reach The Woods. This cabin is way out here. Nothing is close to it. Besides the path, which is barely a path at all with all the hard roots and slippery pine needles all over it, it's like we're in the middle of nowhere. Just out in nature. Far away, I can hear people screaming and talking, ready to start their summer camp experience.

Helen and I dash over the hollow-sounding porch and go inside. It smells like Fritos and sunscreen in here.

I love it.

"Race you to the top bunk!" I yell, running into the closest room.

"No, you don't!" Helen is right behind me. Her long arms grip my shoulder, but I reach forward and slap my hand on the wooden boards of the top bunk at the back of the big, bunkbed-filled room.

"Aw, you beat me," I whine, unable to hold back a

smile. "Not! Are you okay with the bottom bunk?" I hurl my sleeping bag and pillow on the bunk I rightfully won and point to the next one over. Two of the posts almost touch, they're so close. "Or maybe we could both have the top. You could sleep over there."

"It's fine. Whatever," she says, a little annoyed, but I know she won't make a big deal about it. She dumps her stuff on the crackly mattress right below mine. For a second, she doesn't move. That's how I know she's trying to shake off her frustration so we can have a good time.

I'll help her. First, I pop her personal bubble, getting real close. Her lips thin and she leans away from me, but her feet don't move.

"It's tearin' up my heart when I'm with you," I sing. It's the karaoke song we did together last year.

She doesn't look at me, but she grins and follows with the second line. In seconds, we're singing at the top of our lungs and doing the NSYNC choreography in the cramped space between the bunks.

Falling over ourselves with laughter, we finally remember we need to get back to the main camp to find the guys.

Is it weird that nobody else came to set down their sleeping bags to claim a bunk in our room? Maybe they saw us dancing and thought we were two weirdos. I'm sure they'll be here. The cabins always fill up. My first year at camp, I had to wait what felt like an hour just to brush my teeth at night.

Anyway, we smooth our hair, put on a quick dab of lip gloss, and we're out the door.

Ready to get camp started.

3

There's nothing like the first Otter Pop of summer. My mom offered me one a week ago, but I said no because I was waiting to taste one at camp. The red ones are the best. She says the icy treat has a plasticky aftertaste, but that's all part of the experience. Now, I look forward to this signal that today is finally the first day at Camp Oberon.

Helen takes a few more pictures. I can't wait to see how they turn out. Whenever I take pictures, I accidentally ruin half of them by blocking the lens with my hand. She's taking pictures of everybody as they run around or just laugh. We haven't even met most of these campers yet, but we'll get to know each other over the next two weeks, so I guess it's good we'll have photos. My mom lent me her Polaroid camera so I could get some instant pictures to pin up by my bunk.

Something cold and wet touches the back of my arm and I yell, spinning around. Trey stands there, holding a blue Otter Pop. I rub the spot that now has goosebumps. He and Xander are laughing.

"Hey!" I say. It shouldn't hurt that they're laughing. They laugh all the time, but this time it feels weird.

"You jumped so high!" Xander says.

"I didn't jump…"

"Hi, guys," Helen jumps in. She tosses her hair.

"Hey," Trey says.

I cast a look at Helen, since she told me on the bus as a *dead* secret that she has a crush on Trey. I feel the words pressing on the back of my lips, so I bite down on them. I've never talked about crushes. Helen, though, she's loud and fun and way more outgoing than me. I'm not that brave. Usually. Summer camp makes me braver every year, I think as I look up at Xander. His smile is suddenly all I can see and my stomach squirms.

"We're glad we found you," Helen goes on, bringing my attention back to the group again. Her grin makes her crush so obvious.

"Have you seen Robbie?" I ask, and my voice sounds weird.

"Nah, I think he's in a different cabin." Xander scratches the back of his head.

"Which one are you—"

A loud whistle cuts through our conversation. A short, bearded man stands on a picnic table behind us. "Hello, campers, and welcome to Camp Oberon!"

Everyone screams and cheers.

"Listen up, because I have important announcements! First off, nobody should travel alone. Always have a buddy. Your counselors are here to help you with that and anything else you might need while you're here. Wave, counselors!"

Among the crowd, all wearing bright green T-shirts with the 3-D words X-treme Fun, the counselors jump up and down, waving their arms. I chuckle.

"The dining hall is right behind me." He gestures at a big lodge-looking building with steps leading up to the doors. "Every camper gets a map. Bring it in your pocket until you learn where everything is. Uh, lights out at 10:00 every night. And most importantly, have fun!" I clap along with Helen and the boys. "Now," he says, stroking his beard as if he's thinking, "what should we do before pizza?"

"Pizza!" Trey whisper-yells, bumping my shoulder with his.

"Yeah!" Xander exclaims.

Helen gives me a funny look.

The camp director puts his finger in the air like an idea just came to him. "How about a Super Soaker fight?"

I gasp. A Super Soaker fight with this many people would be the bomb! I grip Helen's hand, and that strange feeling I got from her a second ago disappears.

Like magic, neon-colored water guns appear next to the counselors. I reach for one.

"Want to be on my team?" Trey asks.

I didn't realize there were teams. "Sure," I say.

Near us, Xander pumps up his Super Soaker really fast to pressurize the water.

"Do you want to be with us?" I ask him.

"Yeah, man."

My chest swells. The boys don't think I'm a kid after all. Xander and Trey both want to be on a team with me.

Helen's jaw looks tight as she grabs her water gun.

"Come with us," I say. "We'll be the best team ever!"

I am soaking wet and full of pizza by the time it gets dark. A couple people go back to their cabins to shower, but I'd rather shiver in the chilly nighttime air around the kickoff campfire.

The stars look bright above the pointed trees, making the sky almost blue. Smoke and burnt marshmallow tinge the air. I scoot down the log closer to Helen, who wraps

Camp Oberon

one arm around me. Suddenly, I wish that arm belonged to Xander instead.

We're all getting a little tired and cold, so conversations aren't as loud as they were before. This time, the camp director doesn't need to whistle.

"We're going to sing a few Camp Oberon songs," he announces.

I smile. I remember all of them from last year. My fingers encircle the snap bracelet on my wrist.

"Ready?" The camp director sits down, but I lean forward.

I don't how I didn't see him before, but Robbie is sitting right across the campfire from us. He slings a big guitar across his lap.

"Do you like to sing, Mia?"

I turn. Trey's looking at me.

"I do!" Helen says, straightening her back like she's in a choir.

"Eh," Xander grunts. Does he not like the camp songs? I'll just sing quietly, then. "Has Robbie been here the whole time?"

"Right?" I say. "We tried to find him earlier."

Robbie looks older too, more thinned out, like he runs track. But he still has the sparkle in his eye when he lines up his fingers on the strings and raises his eyebrows as if to say hi to us before starting to sing.

"You spotted snakes with double tongue,
Thorny hedgehogs, be not seen;
Newts and blind-worms, do no wrong,
Come not near our fairy queen."

The tune is "Sweet Caroline" but the words are all Camp Oberon. Robbie sings about spiders and beetles and worms, telling them not to bother us campers. The song always makes me laugh. I wish they made a tape of it. Some people talk through the song, but I ignore them.

We sing two more songs. I think my hair is almost dry.

Robbie leans his elbows on his guitar, the shadow of the campfire glowing on its surface. He looks through the smoke at the four of us sitting right across from him. That's when I know he's going to tell a scary story.

"Did you know," he said, "that four campers disappeared from Camp Oberon ten years ago? No one has seen or heard from them since."

I suck in a breath, trying to get ready. What if this story was scarier than last year?

Some of the people sitting on the logs quiet down to listen. Only about half the camp is still here, enough to fill the log benches three deep around this fire. When I saw them setting out a few of those staticky plastic school chairs with the rivets that pull your hair, I made sure our team got a better spot on one of the logs.

"Some people think it was the man with a hook for a hand who wandered through the woods, looking for kids to get out his revenge. A kid accidentally slammed his hand in a door and chopped it off, so now he wants to take the hands of every kid he meets. He still lives in these woods." Robbie scans the darkness behind us.

A shiver shoots up my spine to the back of my neck.

"But I think it was the Puck," he continues. "He kidnapped them from their beds and turned them into something we probably see every day, but don't realize it's the trapped souls of four terrified kids."

I swallow. The Puck again. And I realize that Helen, Xander, Trey, and me make four campers.

"The Puck can do anything," Robbie goes on. "So, if you see a friend in the darkness on your way to your cabin tonight, that could be the Puck. If you hear the water in the lake splash, that's the Puck rising from the waves. If you hear tapping at your window tonight, know that it's the Puck coming to kidnap you."

Tears bite at my eyes. *I will not be a baby.*

Sniffing, I look right back at Robbie. He smirks at me.

The camp director claps his hands and stands. "Well, don't let the Puck get you tonight. Remember, always go in pairs and lights out at 10:00!"

4

The counselors start to shoo us away. I wish we had more time by the fire before I had to walk through the dark woods to our far-off cabin.

"Will you walk us to our cabin?" Helen asks the boys. At least I'm not the only one feeling spooked.

"I will." Xander holds out his hands and we let him pull us to our feet. I don't want to let go of his hand, but he releases me quickly. My skin zings where he touched it. He doesn't talk as much as Trey, but he's more of a gentleman.

My hair falls stringy around my shoulders from the Super Soaker fight earlier, and I suddenly feel cold. Crossing my arms, I walk to the other side of the fire. Robbie is putting his guitar in the hard-shell case.

"Robbie," I say, "where have you been? Did you just get here?"

He clicks the case closed. "Hey, Mia! No, I was here, but I didn't run into you guys."

"How did you not see us? Xander is, like, a thousand feet tall."

He laughs. "Yeah, him and Helen."

I can't help the scowl that forms on my face when he names the two of them together. Does he know something I don't? I glance behind me and Xander's readjusting the sunglasses on his head. The three of them are getting ready to leave.

"Maybe I should go," I say. "Will you meet us for breakfast?"

"I'll walk with you." He stands.

I open my mouth to mention the guitar, but the guitar case has magically vanished. One of the counselors, or maybe the camp director, must have taken it.

"Great!" We catch up to the others, who have already started walking. "I love your guitar playing, by the way," I add.

"Robbie!" Trey greets, wrapping Robbie up in a back-slapping man-hug.

"Where you been, man?" Xander asks, as if we didn't all see him at the campfire.

"Around." Robbie shrugs.

I click on my flashlight. In a second, Helen's beam joins mine. She's not her normal perky self. Something is bothering her.

"Where are we going?" Trey asks.

"Woods," I drone, rolling my eyes. The forest gets blacker and blacker the farther away we get from the dying campfire. Gravel crunches under my tennis shoes.

"Into the woods?" Robbie jumps in front of our flashlights, grinning as he walks backward. "That's where the Puck lives!"

Camp Oberon

"Cut it out, Robbie," Helen says.

"Ooh, yeah, the Puck!" Trey chimes in. Then he leans close to me, wiggling his fingers like he's tickling without actually touching me.

I shove him away. "Stop!"

"Did you say the Woods Cabin?" Xander asks.

I swivel my head. "Yeah?"

"That's where we're staying."

All of us stop dead in the middle of the path.

Xander's and Trey's eyes meet in confusion. I stand closer to Helen. Robbie looks like he's about to burst out laughing.

"Wait," Helen says, "is Woods a boys cabin or a girls cabin this year?"

I pull the camp map out of my pocket and unfold it. "Are you sure that's where you're supposed to be?"

"Yeah, for sure," Trey confirms.

"They have too many campers this year," Robbie explains gleefully. "So they put all the extra people in Woods. Maybe it's gonna be the love cabin." He puckers his lips.

"Stop." I shove him away too.

"What? Like you don't all have crushes on each other? You know what happens when boys and girls get together in a cabin deep in the woods…"

The pepperoni turns in my stomach. *All have crushes?* I fight the urge to cover his mouth. I hate the idea of him guessing who likes who, but I also have to know if Xander likes me back.

Helen pushes past him. "You're the worst, Robbie. Come on."

My heart beats fast as I follow. Are the boys really

going to be in our cabin?

"I can't believe they put the Amazon Middle students in better cabins than us," she fumes.

"Yeah." But I get it. They're older. Every year, there's a feud between the two schools. Every year, I feel sure we're going to win, but then they prank us or take the best food, and we lose.

"Stupid," Xander mutters. But Trey looks almost happy.

I try to catch Xander's eye, but he won't look at me. I cram the map back into my pocket. Xander's not happy about having the cabin so far away. Hopefully, his sour look isn't about spending more time with me.

The guys whip out their own flashlights and walk ahead of us. It's nice to know what's up ahead since our beams together can reach twice as far with them in front. No hint of other campers, but no hint of the hook-handed man or the Puck either.

Robbie stays behind with me and Helen. "They totally like you," he says under his breath.

I pretend not to be interested, but my heartbeat kicks up even faster.

"Who?" Helen asks sharply. "Trey has been following Mia all day. Did he tell you he likes her?"

My mouth falls open. Trey? Liking me? "No," I protest. Helen likes Trey. There's no way he'd like me more than her.

Robbie points at me. "She's right. They both like you." His finger swivels to Helen.

My insides drop.

"Really?" she asks, obviously excited.

"Really. Can't you tell?"

"Well, I don't... Wow!"

I swallow past a lump in my throat. Xander walks confidently up ahead, keeping his flashlight steady while Trey's is pointing all over the place. I thought Xander might see me as more than his kid sister... but that was dumb. Of course he likes Helen instead.

Someone whoops behind us.

I spin around. Three figures stand on the path, hands clawed on either side of their heads. Red devil masks cover their faces.

"Eep!" I cry, almost dropping my flashlight.

The figures run at us, growling.

Helen and I scream. The boys dash to our side.

"Get out of here!" Xander yells.

The devil-masked figures stop right in front of our noses, and I wince. They burst out laughing.

"Amazon Middle rules!"

"They're so lame."

"Chillax, kids. Are you afraid of the Puck coming to eat you?"

They make mocking baby noises, and I have to fight back tears.

"That was mean!" Helen says, putting her hands on her hips. She's as tall as they are.

They just keep laughing.

"Yeah, go away!" Trey echoes.

Finally, the middle schoolers turn and gallop back down the path. At least they aren't in Woods too. I release a breath.

"You girls okay?" Xander asks, looking at me.

For a second, I can't answer. He's looking right at me with those brown eyes. "Yeah," I manage. "We're fine."

"Perfectly fine," Helen echoes, smiling.

That's right. In that second I almost forgot that Xander likes Helen instead of me.

"Wait, where's Robbie?" Trey asks. He swings his light all around the path and the forest beside it. "Did he run, do you think?" He tosses his swoopy hair out of his eyes.

"No way," Xander says. "He did this all the time last year, man. Remember?"

"You don't think he's staying in the Woods too?" I ask.

Helen's thin brows lower. "I don't remember. I don't think he said."

"Wouldn't it be crazy if it was just us?" Trey asks, grinning at me.

"Yeah. Super weird." After what Helen said, it's hard not to notice that Trey keeps looking at me and not her.

What is actually happening?

"It'll be the bomb," Xander says, smiling at me too.

Today has been a whirlwind, with camp starting and the Super Soaker fight and meeting up with camp friends again. That doesn't even count the Amazon Middle jerks or Robbie saying Xander and Trey have crushes on Helen. Plus, we're all in the same cabin.

I have a feeling this will be an interesting night.

I just can't tell Dad.

5

The lake splashes in the distance as the four of us near the cabin. My hair feels crusty and cold from getting soaked earlier. Ahead of us, Xander raises his flashlight so we can see the front porch. Trees like skinny giants bend over its roof. I shiver.

"Let's take a picture in front of the cabin," Helen suggests, getting out her camera.

Any picture taken at night will just be a dark blob once it's developed.

"We could… could point the flashlights at ourselves," I say through chattering teeth.

I don't like the idea—it reminds me of Robbie's scary stories—but at least then we'll get proof that this year at Camp Oberon, we are actually staying with the boys in the same cabin. It feels like we're doing something wrong. And super fun, even if Robbie was the worst by saying that both boys like Helen.

"Mia should take the picture." Trey comes to stand by me as Helen moves a few steps away.

"I got it," she says with a smile.

"Want to use my… my camera?" I offer her the Polaroid. Even if I am freezing and a little jumpy, I'd love a picture with me and the boys.

She tucks the disposable camera under her arm and takes mine. "Yeah, sure. One for me, one for you."

"Perfect." I wrap my arms around my middle, taking a few steps backward toward the cabin so the boys are standing on either side.

"You cold?" Trey asks me.

"I'm fine."

"Take this." He strips off the flannel he's wearing over his T-shirt and hands it to me. The fabric feels warm.

I smile at him, a different kind of warmth heating me up from the inside. "Thanks." I slip it on, and it falls down past my shorts.

"Yeah. No big." He shifts his weight.

"We should carry Mia in the picture," Xander suggests.

What? Usually Trey is the one with ideas like that and Xander is the cool, steady one. Does that mean...?

My mouth catches up with my thoughts. "That would be fun." Hopefully I don't sound as excited as I feel.

"Yeah, sure," Helen says, waving with one hand so we'll hurry up. I wait for her to get annoyed that the boys want to pick me up, but she's cool with it.

I stand awkwardly, stiffly, unsure what to do.

"All right," Trey says. "One, two, three!"

He lifts my top half and Xander holds my legs. I'm glad the darkness hides how hard I'm blushing. My stupid grin is huge.

Snap!

Helen takes the picture with a blinding flash and a click. The boys move to set me down.

"One more!" I say.

Snap!

There goes the second. Xander and Trey ease me to the ground. I totally forgot about shining our flashlights at our faces. At least the camera has a flash. Every time I blink, two big white and green dots get in the way. I hold my arms out, blinded.

"You're gonna run into a tree!" Helen laughs, taking my hand and pulling me up the steps to the porch. "Here." A cool, pointy square is pressed into my palm. The Polaroid. When I blink at it, all I see is white, but our shapes are slowly coming into focus.

Secretly, I hoped Xander would take my hand instead, but that's okay. I keep blinking fast to clear my vision. The longer I can't see straight, the more edgy I get. This forest is nothing like the city. No street lights, no traffic noise, nothing. It must be really late.

I bet the counselors will tell us it's lights out as soon as we step inside.

But they don't.

Because when we go inside, everything is dark and silent. I think it's my eyes at first, but I rub them and blink a few more times. No one has turned on the lights.

"Hello?" Helen yells.

"Hey!" Xander repeats, looking in doorways and up at the ceiling. He directs his flashlight beam around the space. There's a second floor that overlooks this one, with stairs leading up to it at the back of the room, near a tall set of windows looking out into the black forest. Who knew a camp dorm could look so creepy at night, like a haunted house?

I slide the picture into my pocket and try to stay calm.

"Looks like it's just us," Trey says. He smacks the Tasmanian Devil on Xander's chest, obviously stoked.

This feels wrong. "What if they don't know we're up here?" I ask.

"You heard what Robbie said," Xander replies, going over and picking at the camp rules plaque just inside the front door. "They have too many campers this year, man. They know we're here."

Helen wanders back to me from the doorway to our bunks. "The counselor told us this was our cabin. You even asked if we could switch and they said no!"

"Yeah, I did." For some reason, that makes me feel better.

"So it's fine," Trey says, jumping to hit the top of the doorframe to our bunks.

Helen pulls me close to her. "Sleepover!"

"What, you want a pillow fight?" Trey teases.

"Maybe," she says.

Thump!

We freeze.

"What was that?" I squeak.

Xander and Trey go to the window at the far end of the room. "Sounded like it was outside," Xander says.

"What time is it?" Helen checks her watch. She's trying to stay calm too, but I can see she's nervous from her quick breathing. I put a hand on her arm. "Do you think it's the counselor? It's around 10:00."

"Maybe," I say doubtfully.

"Probably nothing," Trey says, returning to us. "Maybe it's those Amazon Middle losers."

"If it's them, we should go and get 'em," Xander says with an angry frown.

Trey hesitates. He almost looks nervous. I've never seen him like that before. "We'll sneak up to their cabin tomorrow night and freak them all out. They'll pee themselves."

"Perfect," Helen says confidently enough to let me breathe again. "'Cause that was mean! They shouldn't scare us like that."

We wait in silence for a second before a muffled clicking sound starts.

"No lights," Xander says, flipping the switch by the door.

Someone turned off the electricity? I turn wide eyes on Helen. She meets my look. Are we going to be attacked? Killed? I wish I hadn't watched reruns of *Are You Afraid of the Dark?* before coming out here...

6

"What do you mean?" Trey runs over to Xander, his flashlight beam zooming crazily, and flips the light switch himself as if that's going to change something.

I catch my breath. "Let's look for other light switches in here. Maybe that one's just broken."

"Good idea, Mia." Helen runs into our room.

I head upstairs.

"I'll go with you," Trey says as he follows me up the creaky steps.

I'm glad I'm not alone. The shadows are darker up here. I glance over the railing. Xander is following me too. My neck heats up and I almost forget why I'm going up here.

"I'll look over here," I say, hoping Trey will take that as a hint to check the other landing so I can search with Xander.

But he just says, "Okay," and sticks closer to me than Putt-Putt and Pep. To tell the truth, I'm not mad that Trey wants to search with me. *Both* guys want to search with me, even though I'm crusty with splashes of mud and Super Soaker water. I need a shower really bad but there is no way I'm doing that in pitch black darkness with the boy I like staying next door. Nuh uh.

"You find it?" Xander calls when he reaches the top of the stairs.

"No," Trey calls back.

All I see is smooth wooden paneling. "Oh wait!" I lunge forward toward a plastic panel on the wall with two switches. I flip them up. Then down. Up and down.

Nothing.

"Looks like the power's out," I say, as casually as I can.

Behind me, Xander huffs.

"We still have our flashlights," Trey says, aiming wildly. I don't like when he does that because it makes the shadows move.

I clear my throat. "Helen, see anything?"

"Nope."

There's a weird silence, and I can tell it's because we don't want to go to bed in our bunks, but we're also too freaked out about the noise to stay together in the big room with the windows looking in.

Finally, Helen heads up the steps. "So what are we doing?"

Trey takes a hackey sack out of his pocket and raises his eyebrows.

"Nah," Xander says.

"How about this?" A folded piece of paper appears in Helen's hand. She must have grabbed it from the room. It has four points with drawings and writing on each of the flaps.

A paper fortune teller. I love those.

"Lame," Trey declares.

Helen juts a hip. "Not if we make it scary."

I clench my teeth. Not more scary stuff! Am I the only one who thinks we're seriously in trouble here?

"How can you make it scary?" Trey points the flashlight at the paper in her hands, making it look white. The window behind her is black. Anyone could see in.

She puts two fingers from each hand under the points so she can flex the fortune teller for the answer to her question. "Choose a number."

"Four," Trey answers.

She opens and closes the origami four times. Holding it out to him, she says, "Now choose one of these numbers."

Four numbers show on the paper flaps. Trey picks the number three.

Helen pauses. "Was that noise somebody trying to get in and eat us?"

I hold my breath.

She unfolds the flap and reads. "100% yes."

It's so quiet after that answer that we can hear our faint, choppy breathing.

"That's stupid," Xander finally says. "They probably all say—"

Smack!

Something hits the window so hard the landing trembles. I scream and grab Trey, who's closest. His heart pounds like crazy.

Xander shines his flashlight beam out the window. Just trees and plants and dirt. But I swear that's where the sound came from.

Something creaks below us on the first floor. I'm too scared to look. Is someone inside? In the corner of my eye, something moves. I can't help it—I glance down. A shadow shaped like a person with a donkey head crosses the floor. I whimper, hiding my face in Trey's shirt.

"What the…" Xander's words die away.

Seconds tick by. I keep expecting noises on the stairs. Or a scream.

But it's quiet for a long time.

Trey's hold on me tightens. He's wrapped his arms around my back. Forcing my breathing to slow down, I untangle myself from him. If Xander hadn't been standing over there, I would have hung onto him instead.

When I meet Helen's eyes, she's glaring at me. But it's not like I wanted to hug Trey. He was just there. It was an emergency. Did she not see the monster shadow?

Xander swings his flashlight back to Helen. "Does it say what's trying to get us?"

"It can only answer yes or no questions," she says in a breathless voice. Now even Helen, who likes spooky stuff, sounds scared.

"Is it the kids from Amazon Middle?" he asks.

She has him pick the numbers his time. When she lifts the flap to read the answer, it's a no.

"Then what the heck is it?" Trey demands. He's gotten louder, which means he's freaked out. At first, I felt excited that there was no counselor in the cabin, but now I wish one was here.

Helen looks at Trey. "Why don't you and Xander go and see? You have to keep me safe."

"And Mia," Xander adds, warming my belly. I catch his eye and he's looking back at me. If I could drown in his eyes, I would.

Helen's gaze jumps around at the three of us. "But I know you like me and not Mia."

Her words slice me open like a knife. "Helen! What the heck?" Why would she say something like that in front of them? Anger and embarrassment flush away almost all my fear.

"No way, man," Xander says.

My heart jumps with hope, but Helen looks really upset.

"Robbie told us you both have huge crushes on me," she protests, letting the paper fortune teller dangle from one hand.

Trey frowns. "He told us that you didn't want to hang out with us anymore. He said Mia really liked one of us, though, and we had to figure out which one. You just hung around because of Mia."

"Yeah," Xander says. "Why don't you want to hang out with us?"

"I do!" Her eyes look red in the bright beam of the flashlight, but I don't feel sorry for her. She has broken our friendship by making me sound like I'm nothing.

"You obviously don't want to hang out with me," I tell her, my voice breaking. "That was a secret."

"Robbie didn't say it was a secret," she shoots back. "Want to know a real secret?" She looks at the boys.

My guts freeze.

"Mia likes Xander."

7

My mouth falls open. "Helen!" I push her and the origami falls from her hand.

"You like me?" Xander asks.

I'm too mortified to answer or even look at him. "I can't believe you said that! I never told you anything."

She raises her chin, all smug. I thought we were friends. Guess not.

"Helen likes Trey!" I blurt.

She gasps. "You little troll!"

"You skinny beanpole!"

"Hey, hey!" Xander holds out his hands. "Mia… that's cool."

I whirl. Is he saying what I think he's saying?

Both guys are looking at us. I can't read their expressions, and not just because it's dark.

"That's cool," Xander repeats. A little smile creeps onto his face.

Air gusts from my lungs. "Really?"

"Yeah."

Trey steps forward. "You seriously like me, Helen?"

My friend crosses her arms and looks away, close to tears. Now I do feel a little bad. I don't want her to feel totally left out.

"Helen…" I reach for her hand. She doesn't take it. "My bad. I shouldn't have said that."

She just nods. She owes me an apology too, but she's not saying it.

Xander bumps Trey's shoulder. Trey tosses his hair out of his eyes, looking more uncomfortable than I've ever seen him. "Is it true, though?" he asks again.

She raises her eyes, mouth turned down. "Maybe."

That means yes.

Trey beams, smiling so wide I can see his tongue. "Helen, you're the coolest. I thought you'd never… Ha!"

Now, I'm standing near Xander and Trey stands near Helen. Nothing outside seems half so scary as it did a second ago. Not even the Puck.

Even though I try to stop it, a yawn splits my face. All three of them yawn too.

"Should we all bring our stuff to the main room?" Xander asks, scratching the back of his neck shyly. He's so cute when he's flustered.

"Yeah!" I agree.

Monster or no monster, I'm tired now, and I want me

and Helen and the boys to be all together. We hurry down the stairs. Helen and I run into the room with our bunks. As I grab my *Lion King* sleeping bag, I catch her eye. "Friends?"

She squeezes my hand. "Best friends forever."

"Don't call me names again."

"Don't call *me* names."

We giggle.

In a minute, we've joined the guys in the middle of the big room, our sleeping bags rolled out in a row. My sleeping bag really is the best, not kiddish at all. We girls set up in the center, the boys on the ends. I listen for more tapping or bangs on the windows, but no more scary noises interrupt our night. In the morning, we'll investigate what the heck happened.

In the dark, Xander threads his fingers through mine. I smile, and it feels like nothing can get us.

———

At breakfast the next morning, I stuff pancakes and Go-Gurt into my mouth. I think about getting a bowl of Lucky Charms too, because my parents never buy sugary cereals even though they taste amazing.

Sitting around me at the round table are Xander, Helen, and Trey. I never did end up taking a shower, so I'm wearing a ponytail with a baseball cap today. Xander doesn't mind. He's been stuck to my side all morning. I hope it stays like this forever. Dad will for sure see what an incredible guy Xander is. Right now, though, I'll keep it a secret, like the fact the four of us are living in Woods by ourselves.

Trey gives Helen a quick kiss on the cheek, and she blushes.

"Why do you think Robbie told us the wrong thing last night?" I ask before taking a sip of Tang.

"He doesn't know what he's talking about, man," Xander says.

Helen sits up. "Where is Robbie?"

I scan the dining hall. Deer and mountain goat heads, along with peasants on branches—all taxidermy—line the wall near the ceiling. There's a big wooden sign that's been painted green over the main door that says Camp Oberon Dining Hall. The room is filled with kids so it's super loud. Silverware clinks, feet stomp over the boarded floor, and the whole place smells like pancakes and bacon.

But no Robbie. Every time I think I hear his laugh, he isn't there.

"Is he gone again?" Trey rolls his eyes. "Maybe *he* doesn't want to hang out with us."

"I'm sure he does," Helen says. "We spent the whole summer with him last year. Why would he suddenly ditch us?"

"Maybe we can ask a counselor which cabin he's in. Maybe he slept in." I shrug.

A girl in a bright green counselor shirt and high blonde ponytail walks by with a plate of bacon and eggs.

I clear my throat. "Excuse me."

She doesn't hear me.

"Hey!" Xander says. She finally stops and turns around. "We need to know what cabin our friend is in."

Her eyes look irritated that we stopped her, but she plasters a smile on her face. "Who's your friend?"

"Robbie."

She sets her plate down on our table and fishes in her pocket. "Do you know his last name?"

I rack my brain. He said it one time, but I don't remember.

She pulls out a folded sheet of paper, like a fancier version of the maps we all got, and waits for an answer.

I look at Xander. He has a pretty good memory, I think. But it's Helen who says, "Goodfellow."

The counselor squints at the back of her paper for an awkwardly long time. Finally, she shakes her head. "Good one! You almost got me."

"What do you mean?" I ask, as she folds the paper back up.

"There's no camper named Robbie Goodfellow. You've been listening to too many stories. Robbie, Robin... Got it."

Helen cocks her head. "We saw him last night."

"The Puck? Oooh, scary!" She picks up her plate again. Her smile is gone.

How does she know something scary happened at the Woods? A shiver rinses down my back.

"He was here," Trey insists. "And what do you mean, 'the Puck'?"

"Robin Goodfellow is another name for the Puck. I'm gonna have my breakfast now." She turns to leave.

The four of us stare at each other. No camper named Robbie? Another name for the Puck?

Was Robbie the one who scared us last night? Was he the one who made sure only the four of us would be assigned to that faraway cabin?

The pancakes flip over inside me. But along with shock, I feel something else.

Excitement.

Carly Stevens

This has already been the most radical summer ever at Camp Oberon, and it's only just started. I still have two more weeks with my best friends.

I grin, even though I'm still a tiny bit freaked out. No one has a camp story better than this. Too bad no one will ever believe it.

That reminds me. I never saw that picture Helen took of me and the boys. It was too dark by the time I remembered it last night. I pinch the edge and pull it out of my pocket. The photo is only slightly crinkled.

In the center, I'm beaming as Trey and Xander hold me up. Trey's skin glows bright in the flash, making Xander harder to see. I run my thumb down the picture next to Xander's handsome face.

Then my eyes widen. In the background is the black, hazy outline of the cabin porch and roof. But I swear there's another figure back there. It's next to the cabin wall, in the woods, barely a wisp.

I lean over to Helen. "Is that...?" I don't even know how to ask it.

"Yeah," Xander says, looking over my shoulder. "Is that a person?"

"A person?" Helen narrows her eyes. "Oh my gosh!"

"What?" Trey demands, jumping from his seat to stand behind me for a better look.

"Look!" I say, pointing.

It's not quite a whole body, but it's definitely someone laughing.

And we all know who it is.

transcript of police interview [horatio flite]

. . .

Southern Crime (Hamlet)

ELSINORE DEPARTMENT OF PUBLIC SAFETY
BUREAU OF CRIMINAL APPREHENSION
TRANSCRIPT
INTERVIEW DATE: 2 JUNE 2008
CASE #: 4167
OFFENSE: MULTIPLE HOMOCIDE
INTERVIEW OF: HORATIO FLITE
INTERVIEWED BY: SA HANSON FORT JR.

SA FORT: It is at this time 16:30 in the afternoon on the second of June, 2008. This is Special Agent Hanson Fort Jr. I'm here with Officer Abel English and today I'll be interviewing Horatio Flite in Room 204 of the Elsinore County Police Department. Mr. Flite has elected not to have an attorney present.

HORATIO: That's right.

SA FORT: Very good. Very good. You know you can call

off this interview whenever you please. You are free to come and go. Officer English read you your rights?

Horatio: [nods]

SA Fort: We need a verbal affirmation.

Horatio: Yes.

SA Fort: Very good. Now, we want to ask you some questions, just to get at the heart of the truth about these events. We haven't had the opportunity to speak before this, Horatio. Your name is Horatio? I've been let to know it is.

H: Yes.

SA: And how do you spell that? Your whole name, that is.

H: H-O-R-A-T-I-O F-L-I-T-E

SA: Oh, so it's not like the bird, then?

H: Not like the bird.

SA: Horatio. That's a name that just rolls off the tongue, don't it? You go by the full name? Not... well, I guess Ratio isn't a common nickname but— [laughs]

H: The whole thing.

SA: Okay, Horatio. I understand you're a student?

H: Yes.

SA: Where?

H: Witt State College

SA: State College? You look like a university man to me. Must be those elbow patches. Forgive me. Forgive me. Just making observations.

H: Okay.

SA: What are you studying?

H: Literature.

SA: Do you like it?

H: I did.

Transcript of Police Interview [Horatio Flite]

SA: You say that in the past tense, Horatio. Do you not intend to return or do you not like literature anymore?

H: I don't know.

SA: I read some books in college. Interesting stuff. *Beowulf*, Bradbury… Do you have a favorite?

H: [inaudible]

SA: What was that?

H: *The Brothers K. The Brothers Karamazov.*

SA: Oh, philosophical! Dark, I think I heard. Isn't that one a murder mystery as well?

H: The father gets… murdered.

SA: I see. I see. Do you like those kinds of books in general?

H: Murder mysteries?

SA: Yes.

H: Not usually.

SA: Well, I guess that's as smooth a segue as we're going to get to the events of May 29. Do you remember where you were on May 29, 2008?

H: I was at… the Dane residence.

SA: The Dane residence. Yes. Had you been there before?

H: Many times.

SA: How were you connected to that family?

H: Henry Dane… I'm sorry. Henry Dane and I were friends. Close friends.

SA: How did you know each other?

H: We met in college freshman year. We lived in the same dorm and had a couple classes together. I'd heard of him before that.

SA: When?

H: His family's famous, obviously, at least in Elsinore

County. I don't follow politics most of the time, but I was pretty happy with Roy Dane when he was governor. I mean, nobody's perfect. But most of us like him around here. All the kids would go trick or treating at their house because it was big and kind of scary, but it had the best candy.

SA: So you've known where the Dane manor resides for a long time?

H: Yes.

SA: Know any of the others?

H: Not personally. Well, I talked to Mrs. Dane, Gloria Dane, a couple times.

SA: Were you friends too?

H: I wouldn't say so. But she's a hostess, so she knows how to talk to people. Have you never talked to her?

SA: Who were you there to see or what were you there to do on the evening of May 29?

H: I'd been staying there.

SA: Staying there?

H: I was going to stay for the summer.

SA: With Henry, or…?

H: Yes. His family let me stay.

SA: I imagine they must have a lot of guest rooms.

H: [inaudible]

SA: Which room were you residing in? Could you draw it out for me?

H: [draws a partial map of the Dane residence with an X over one room]

SA: This was your personal retreat? Anyone else staying in that room with you?

H: All the time, no.

SA: So, back to the evening of May 29. Do you

Transcript of Police Interview [Horatio Flite]

remember what happened then? Walk us through it, if you'd be so kind.

H: Henry has another friend, um, Luther, who offered to come over and shoot clay targets.

SA: Luther invited himself?

H: I'm actually not sure. We were talking about it by lunchtime and then he came over around three.

SA: Always planning to shoot clay targets, or did they devise that plan after he arrived?

H: That's why he was coming over. Luther and Henry both shoot.

SA: Have you ever done that?

H: I tried it once. I'm not very good. I grew up most of my life in Connecticut, on the coast, and nobody did any shooting sports that I knew.

SA: Why did you decide to come down south to a state college, then?

H: Roots, I guess. I don't know.

SA: Because you grew up here?

H: Yes.

SA: When did you move to Connecticut?

H: When I was nine.

SA: Ah, go on.

H: Luther came over to shoot with Henry, you know, in the backyard. They have all that property. They have a clay pigeon launcher even. I don't know what those things are called.

SA: Damned if I do either. Pardon my French.

H: We all went out to watch. Um…

SA: Take your time. Take your time. Did Luther bring his own firearm?

H: [clears throat loudly] I think so. Yes.

SA: And what did Henry use?

H: One from his family's collection. They keep them out in the shed. I'm sure you've already seen that.

SA: Do you know how many guns they have?

H: I don't know. I'm not a gun guy. I didn't touch any of them.

SA: Did they shoot clay targets that day?

H: Yes.

SA: How many, would you say if you had to hazard a guess?

H: Eight, maybe.

SA: Did they seem like they knew what they were doing?

H: Yes. They both took lessons at some point. They're very good.

SA: They weren't waving the firearms around, for instance?

H: Henry would never do that.

SA: What about Luther?

H: He…

SA: Take your time, Horatio. I'm simply trying to unravel what happened. I'll be honest with you, son. We found gunpowder residue on everyone, not just the two boys. So that leaves me wondering how that could have happened. Can you shed any light for me?

H: [doesn't answer]

SA: Do you remember what happened that day?

H: The residue on me… That was probably Henry's.

SA: All right. How would that have happened?

H: It took him… a couple minutes… after he was shot.

SA: Are you saying you tried to help Henry?

H: I couldn't help him. There was nothing I could do.

Transcript of Police Interview [Horatio Flite]

SA: So how would gunpowder have transferred to your person, do you think?

H: Um. Luther shot him. And I... [clears throat] I couldn't... I held him up so he could maybe breathe better.

SA: You held him up?

H: Mm hm.

SA: Could you demonstrate?

H: Like this, I guess. [gestures holding a supine person partially upright against his chest]

SA: Officer English, would you get this young man a drink of water? Is there anything else you'd like? We have bad coffee and a vending machine with Fritos and the like. Haha. No? All right. Just water.

English: [exits]

SA: I'm sorry I have to ask you all these questions, Horatio. Officer English told me how he found you. Recounting these events would be taxing for anyone.

H: Officer Fort?

SA: Special Agent. That's all right. Go on.

H: Are you still recording?

SA: No. [sound of buttons being touched but not fully pressed] Not at this precise time.

H: I think I remember you.

SA: Remember me?

H: Being around the Danes.

SA: They're a prominent family, son. They have many people around them. I've never been intimate with that family, so to speak.

H: Or... there was something. Maybe Henry mentioned you.

SA: I'd be flattered.

H: Or Roy.

SA: Did you know him?

H: It's... yes.

SA: Under what circumstances, if you don't mind my asking?

H: Henry, again.

SA: Ah. So you knew him before—

H: Before everything, yeah. We'd known each other a little while.

SA: When you say everything...

H: I mean when Roy Dane died.

SA: Of course, of course. Terrible blow to everyone. Terrible surprise.

H: It was.

SA: How did Henry take that turn of events?

H: We... It was hard for him.

SA: Were you close then too? You said you were staying there this summer.

H: We... yeah. That's about when... That was just after we really become friends, you know?

SA: So you had the heartbreaking privilege to see his grief up close, so to speak?

H: If that's how you want to put it.

SA: Did he act differently?

H: Well, yeah, of course. He lost his dad. He wouldn't get out of bed some days. There was a week when we just drank Mountain Dew and watched *Golden Girls* and James Bond, like, back and forth. That's... stupid. But yeah, he really had a hard time.

SA: That certainly sounds like it. Did he ever mention harming himself or others at that time?

H: I'd rather not answer that. Not others.

SA: Himself, then?

Transcript of Police Interview [Horatio Flite]

H: None of this was his fault.

SA: I didn't say so, didn't suggest it.

H: You keep trying to suggest it, and I'm telling you this wasn't his fault.

SA: Okay. I'm listening to you.

H: Roy. You knew Roy. He talked about you.

SA: Haha, I don't think—

H: It was... mail on the counter, and I overheard him saying something to Mrs. Dane. The house. You wanted the house.

SA: It's a fine house, but—

H: Yes, something about the property. They said you were harassing them.

SA: Horatio, I'm not the one being questioned here. I didn't know that family, but looks like you did, so we're both trying to find answers.

H: Did you have something to do with this?

SA: Haha, how might that have come about? This tragedy occurred before your very eyes, or did it not?

H: It was... There was just so much craziness.

SA: Take a couple deep breaths. The water's here. [sound of fumbled buttons again]

[Officer English enters]

SA: We're resuming at 17:10. Thank you, Officer. The young man needs a moment.

H: I don't need a moment. You were harassing them, the Danes.

SA: Do you have any proof about your person? Now, Horatio, I've not hurled unsubstantiated accusations at you, despite the circumstances under which you were found. I'd thank you kindly not to hurl them at me.

H: Do you accuse me?

SA: Beg pardon?

H: Do you think I hurt the Danes?

SA: You have no motive to hurt the Danes, that I can divine.

H: You think I killed Luther?

SA: Such boldness. And here, I thought you were a soft-spoken sort of young man.

H: You didn't say no.

SA: I strive for honesty in all things.

H: Then can you answer my question? Did you harass the Danes? Do you have anything to gain from all this? Does it benefit you?

SA: The unfortunate and untimely deaths of four people? I'll thank you to keep to the topic.

H: You'll buy the house, won't you? That property that's worth millions.

SA: As if I have millions to spend…

H: Stop, Agent Fort. You've wanted the Dane property and their reputation for years. I remember Roy—

SA: You remember nothing, young man. These deaths have nothing to do with me. Perhaps they have something to do with you.

H: No. It was all a bunch of accidents. Some of them were accidents. I would never hurt Henry.

SA: Luther?

H: No. I didn't even know him. I'm not saying you were there. I'm just saying you benefit from this whole thing happening. You don't mind what's happened. You don't mind that Henry is gone.

SA: Henry was a fine young man. Would have proven a most honorable type of person had he been given the chance.

Transcript of Police Interview [Horatio Flite]

H: Yes.

SA: I liked Henry, what I knew of him.

H: You don't know anything about him.

SA: That's probably true. Here, I'm just going to leave this pad and pen here with you and Officer English. I don't see that it's fruitful for me to remain at this moment. We still need to know what happened at that residence. Kindly write down all you can remember. Include dates and details, if you would.

H: I'll find that letter.

SA: Horatio.

H: I'll prove you benefit from all this. That's why you need this statement from me.

SA: Officer English will walk you through it.

H: To prove you have nothing to do with what happened. You asked to be on this case, didn't you?

SA: I think the interview's about wrapped up.

H: You did. Just to cover yourself. See what they know.

SA: Illuminati will be the next thing out of your mouth.

H: Search the house, Officer English. You'll find proof. There's some connection.

SA: Good day, Mr. Flite.

[SA Fort exits]

what you will
. . .
Winter Cottagecore (Twelfth Night)

I HAD HEARD of Orsino before coming to live in Illyria. Two years earlier, before the incident with my brother, I had gone to see one of his performances at King Edward University. He played the lead role with such pathos that, of course, I fell instantly in love with him. The next day, I switched my concentration to poetry. Perhaps it's a good thing that my parents are dead.

So, by November, when suspicion followed me everywhere and all I could see were traces of my twin in the dorm, in our car, in my classes, I resolved to escape. Losing a brother is hard enough without constant interrogation. Even my voice classes and books of poetry weren't enough to lose myself in. I had to get away.

King Edward University, tucked into the thick trees of New England far from my California home, felt right. Besides, Orsino was there.

I'd dabbled in drama myself, singing in a couple musicals, but always too awkward to score the lead roles. That experience gave me knowledge of stage makeup and disguise, though. When I say I wanted a fresh start, I wanted more than just a new place. I wanted a new identity. I wanted to leave one life for a new one, keeping only the sweet memory of Sebastian tucked away in a corner of my mind where no one could reach it.

I made the transfer over winter break. The official university records had my real name—Viola—but I wrote my new name on everything else. I was Cesar. Hair short, breasts bound, voice deepened, I moved into Illyria, the men's house on campus.

At first, the others weren't sure what to make of me, but, in true drama kid fashion, they teased me into their inner circle. A small, androgynous, Mexican poetry major obsessed with music and drama.

Over Christmas, I haunted the great house alone. It had a main staircase and a servant staircase, wonky garlands draped over the bannisters, scuffed and scored wood floors, masks on the wall, a corner with instruments, a shelf with booze, and a fireplace. The couch in front of the fireplace was stained enough that I only sat on pillows while the others were gone. And books. Cases full of scripts and pulpy detective novels and ancient philosophy.

My brother's drowning had made me more melancholy than I'd ever been in my life. Illyria, with Orsino in it, started to inject life in me again. Even Christmas Day wasn't as dreary as it could have been. I made salty cookies shaped like partridges and pears, danced to David Bowie, and saw how far I could slide across the floor in my socks.

The approach of next term had me a bit worried, though. Would the other students see through Cesar to

Viola? Would they say, "Isn't that the girl who…?" I couldn't stand it if they did.

"Play that again," Orsino said, stretching out on the couch in front of the fireplace.

Only the two of us had returned so far after New Year's. I didn't realize he'd been listening as I tinkered on the piano. That morning, I'd caught my own reflection in the antique glass above the mantel, and the resemblance I bore to my brother struck me with huge force. This song was some of my thoughts to him made music.

"This?" I asked, replaying the last series of notes.

"That's it," he said languorously. "What is it?"

"I'm just… playing around."

"Hmm." The deep, throaty noise made my stomach twist. "I like it. It has a dying fall."

"A dying fall," I echoed, tasting the words. Orsino would probably make a better poet than I was. I played the melody one more time.

"That's enough," he said, sitting up and setting the book in his hand aside. "You can sing too, right?"

"I… yes." My alto had become a tenor I wasn't fully used to, but I still sang.

He sighed. When he sighed, I saw all the lovers in great poems. He was fit and lithe and picturesque, with pale skin and hair almost as dark as mine. Emotions beamed through his eyes, clear as light, even from a distance. It was that more than anything that struck me when I saw him perform.

I cleared my throat gruffly, unsure of what to do.

"Olivia." He said the name as though it were chocolate. "She hasn't accepted any of my letters, she won't let me visit, she won't answer the door."

I drooped. Olivia's name fluttered like fresh snow over everything. She sounded like a mythical creature, a perfect fairy woman. Half the house was in love with her. I'd never seen so much as a picture. Others praised her, but Orsino was allowed to pine after her. He, as the most frequent dramatic lead, was the de facto leader of the house. When there was a party, he hosted, despite the fact that eleven more of us lived there.

"She says she won't date for the rest of college—that's a year and a half—all because of her brother."

"What about her brother?" The question came out high-pitched and I forced my hands not to cover my mouth. This wasn't information I'd heard before. Most of the talk circled around how beautiful she was or the shows she'd been in.

"He died a few months ago."

Tears stung my eyes.

Catching my emotion, Orsino gave a rueful smile. "We still get to live, though, right?"

I couldn't speak. That is what I was trying to do, assuming a different identity, a different gender, a different life. But here was someone I longed for, and he longed for this Olivia, who shouldn't be rushed through her grief.

"Would you sing to her?"

"What?" My voice cracked on the syllable. I brought my register down. "What are you talking about?"

"From me. I want to see her happy. I want us to go out sometime, and her friends won't even open the door for me."

"You want me to go to Countess House?" It was a large cottage-style building about half a mile away from Illyria.

King Edward campus wasn't particularly large, so I'd developed an internal map quickly.

"Would you?" He turned those blazing eyes on me with pleading in them.

"To sing?"

"Or recite poetry. You're studying that, right?"

"Mmmm, right. And say it's from you?"

The yearning expression on his face transformed into amusement. "Are you that uncomfortable, Cesar?"

"No. I can... I can do that." It was pathetic, but this was a way to solidify the closeness we were beginning to build, so I had to do it, even if it meant he wooed Olivia through me. The idea sent my head spinning.

Orsino rose, clapping me on the back. "Thanks. I really do like that song." He walked away humming it.

A sprawling trellis climbed the height of the wall, covered in spindly branches topped with snow. As I approached, shoes soaked in snow-water, nerves gripped me. Olivia probably wouldn't let me in, but what if she did? What if I had to sing? My throat felt raw from the cold. Even my lips numbed over my scarf. Brown plaid trousers and a thick blue sweater weren't protection enough from the cold.

The door, made of vertical panels painted teal, looked like the entrance to a fairy cottage—feminine and cozy, the kind of door I'd like to come across randomly after wandering in a foreign place. There would surely be muffins and flowers and tea within.

Hot tea sounded heavenly now. I knocked, the glove muffling the sound.

Since most students were still gone for Christmas holiday, the grounds felt abandoned, smothered in silence. I felt like the traveler in Guy de Maupassant's poem, listening in vain for hushed watchers to respond.

No one answered. I removed my glove and knocked again.

A pert girl with long auburn curls opened the door. Her frosty look thawed upon seeing me, probably nothing but a dollop of wool in the snow.

"Hello," I attempted through my scarf. "I'm here to see Olivia."

"Who are you?"

From what I understood, Olivia had sworn off men, not women, but I'd chosen my path and would stick to it, even if reverting to my former identity would make entrance easier. I was Viola and Cesar. One day I might return, but not now. Not when I'd just managed to start something new.

I wavered at the thought of muffins.

"Cesar. I live in Illyria."

"She's not available."

When the girl tried to close the door, I held it open with my shoe. "What's your name?" I asked.

"Mary." She arched a red brow at me.

"Please, Mary, I need to speak with her. It's freezing out here. Please, just let me in."

"Who is that?" A dark-skinned girl interjected, poking her head through the crack in the door, a full head taller than Mary.

"It's fine, Fable. I've taken care of this," Mary said, looking up at her.

"Tell her I'm here," I shouted through the opening, hoping Olivia would hear me herself. "I'll just stand here in the cold until she gets back or will talk to me." I lowered my voice, sounding so much like Sebastian that the words almost hitched. "I know she's been through a hard time lately. I don't want to make it worse. I just want to talk to her."

Mary and Fable looked at each other, skeptically at first, then softly. Maybe I was able to project my desperation through dewy-eyed looks like Orsino could after all.

Mary swung open the door and Fable stepped aside to let me pass. Grateful, I tromped over the threshold into the warmth. As soon as I lowered my scarf, the smell of moss and vanilla wafted up. White and pink flowers stood in vases, a living answer to the white outside. The furniture was cushy, the lights ambient and warm. The slight dustiness of sadness lay over everything.

I removed my other glove, aware I was dripping moisture onto the thick carpet.

"We'll... tell her you're here," said Mary with a quirk of her lips that suggested she already regretted letting in this stranger. As she bustled away, her long, pale pink skirt flounced up to show thick socks pulled halfway up her calves.

"What do you want to talk to her about?" Fable asked as soon as Mary was out of the room. We stood eye to eye. I'd always been tall myself.

"I... I would like to sing... to her."

Squiggly lines formed on Fable's forehead and the corner of her eyes creased. "You sing too?"

Not the response I'd been expecting. I released a cold breath, working at the buttons of my heavy coat. "Yes. I enjoy it. I take lessons."

"But you're new here."

It wasn't a question. King Edward's was small enough that it wasn't difficult to spot someone out of place. "I'm going to take lessons again when the term starts."

"You look a little familiar, though."

I froze, fingers still on the final button. "No. No, I'm sure we haven't met," I muttered, forcing myself to move. Had the headlines reached this far east?

"Do you play soccer?"

"No."

"Live in town?"

"I…"

Mary returned and I practically jumped into her arms with relief. The girl stiffened at my apparent joy to see her. "Olivia says you can visit her. But make it quick."

"Great!" I bypassed Fable and skipped in the direction Mary had come from. "Right down here?"

To my irritation, both girls followed me down the hall to a dimly lit bedroom. A handmade wooden plate on the door said "Olivia."

"Hello?" I said quietly, politely, as I went inside.

Three girls sat among a thousand white and gray cushions. Strings of black and white photographs festooned the walls artfully.

"Um, which one is Olivia?" I whispered to Mary, who stood by me. The room was so quiet that there was no way everyone didn't hear me. My face flushed hot at my ignorance.

"What do you want to say to her?" asked a mellifluous voice. The owner of the voice was a pale girl with delicate features and large, wise eyes. With her wild brown hair and alluring aspect, she seemed a forest creature. She wore a corduroy dress the color of charcoal over a collared white shirt, one knee drawn up as she lounged on the white-quilted bed.

"Are you Olivia?" I asked, louder.

"I can speak for her."

I glanced at the other girls sitting around the room. None of them struck me as the type who would capture Orsino's heart so completely except for this fairy creature.

"I have something to tell you, if you are her," I said.

"Go ahead." She canted her head curiously. Definitely Olivia, then.

I thought of the song I'd prepared, but my breath stuck in my throat. "I can't do it with all these people watching. It's for your ears only."

"Intriguing."

No one moved to leave.

"The words come from Orsino, who loves you," I said, summoning my courage. "I can't let all these people mock the secret longings of a love-sick heart." My drama background came in handy with that little speech. I felt taken out of myself.

Olivia's dark eyebrows rose. "Are you a comedian?"

"No," I said indignantly. Unless I counted the two farcical roles I'd played last year...

Olivia looked around at her entourage. Obviously, she was the Orsino of this house. "I'll be all right," she said, prompting them to go.

Relief mixed with the tension I felt at this backwards mission of performing for a grieving girl just because I wanted a boy to notice me. And I didn't even know if Orsino liked boys. It was a knot as tangled as my stomach.

The girls filed out like novitiates in a convent. I felt Fable's eyes linger on me the longest.

Olivia slid upward on the bed until she rested with her back against the headboard. "Now, what are these 'secret longings'?"

"Orsino loves you."

"You don't say."

Her cavalier dismissal of Orsino's interest grated for a moment, but I recovered. "He asked if I would present something for you."

"Oh, yes?"

"A song."

Her pink mouth pursed with amusement. "Let's hear it."

I raised my chin, sending a few droplets of cold water left clinging to my short hair sliding down the back of my neck.

"A great while ago the world begun,
With hey, ho, the wind and the rain..."

"How long is this song?"

I blinked in surprise. I'd barely started. "It's... I don't know. Four minutes long?" It was one of the last showcase pieces I'd prepared at my previous school.

"I've heard it. The lovesick man tries to hide from all the evils of the world but he falls into the clutches of love. She doesn't love him back. He dies alone. It's a sad tale."

A little put out, I stepped forward. "Are you sure you don't want to hear it? I've been practicing all morning."

"Do you have anything else?" She was teasing me now, openly.

"I'm telling you that Orsino loves you with sighs and groans and… he suffers for you." A twinge echoed in my own heart.

"Little me?" She tapped her pointed chin with a finger. The slightest edge, like black ice, slicked her words with desperation instead of humor. She was trying to stave off her sadness. Past her, the black and white photographs all had a young man in them.

"I see why he does," I said. "You're beautiful. You're special."

"What parents say to unwanted children. Lovely."

"I mean it." I took another step forward. Maybe my proximity would get her to hear me, to be comforted by Orsino's love. "I've rarely seen a beauty like yours." And it was true. Painters would envy her for a muse. I wished fleetingly that I had any skill in the visual arts myself. She would be the perfect siren, wood nymph, pixie, sprite.

"Ah, my beauty," she teased. "I'll just write it down so he can find someone else with my features. Don't worry. I won't leave out a thing." Her eyes sparkled with venomous mischief as she propelled herself off the bed and leaned toward me. "Or you can get out a pen as I dictate." She cleared her throat delicately, pointing as she inventoried. "Two lips, somewhat red. Two gray eyes, with lids to them. One neck, one chin—"

"There's no need to mock me." I'd had enough of that. But in her mockery I sensed an underlying grief. "I see what you are," I continued, gentler, my eyes flitting to the photographs. "You're proud. I was just trying to help. To lift your spirits because someone loves you.

Imagine what Orsino's going through since you won't talk to him."

She gave me a steely look. "What is he going through?"

"If I loved you like he does, I would build a willow cabin outside your gate just so I could see you passing by. Your beauty would burn, but I'd be glad to burn if it meant I could be near you. I'd write new mythologies and poetry to immortalize your life on paper. Every night, I'd sigh and pray you'd look at me again, but differently." I gently took her upper arms. The way she looked back at me now meant she was hearing what I said. I was getting through to her. And the force of that gaze made me understand Orsino better. "I'd memorize your name on my tongue until the wilderness itself echoed it back to me." I finished on a dry-mouthed whisper.

She kept staring with the glittery gray of foxes and nuthatches. Wonder and anticipation and wariness.

I released her arms.

She blinked, the spell broken. Turning her face from mine, she gave a dry chuckle. "You might actually get somewhere." Her elfin eyes flashed up to mine again. "What's your name again?"

"Cesar."

"Where are you from?"

"California."

She sighed, an echo of the one I'd heard that morning. "Tell Orsino that I can't love him and I don't want to talk to him. You could… tell me how he takes it."

"If that's your answer, then there's no need for me to come back."

"I'm sorry you came all this way in the cold."

I shrugged, even though I dreaded the freezing walk back. "All right then…"

"Stay!"

The command was so sudden that I almost tripped over my feet the short distance to the door. I turned.

Olivia stood there, wild-haired and pink-cheeked, classic as a statue. "Have a muffin. And tea. Just until you warm up."

I smiled. I'd been right after all.

She smiled back. She really was beautiful. But something in that look gave me pause. I couldn't parse it at first, but as she swept out to fetch the snacks without allowing the others back in, and as we sat on the floor to drink the tea, and as she laughed without the black-ice grief, I realized.

I had charmed her.

Me.

As Cesar.

A riot of emotions stirred at the realization. I was happy, flattered to have caught the interest of someone so dazzling, thankful I could assuage her grief a moment, curious, and—loud above it all—dreading the news I had to take back to Illyria. Olivia didn't like Orsino. She liked me.

"You can finish that song now," she said.

I raised an eyebrow. I couldn't help picturing Orsino and Olivia together on stage. They'd be iconic. I would watch every show and hurt in the audience. "Are you sure you want me to?"

"I was rude earlier. Yes."

I set down my tea and began.

Carly Stevens

> *"But when I came to man's estate,*
> *With hey, ho, the wind and the rain.*
> *'Gainst knaves and thieves men shut their gate,*
> *For the rain it raineth every day.*
> *But that's all one, our play is done,*
> *And we'll strive to please you every day."*

to have had so much blood

. . .

Gothic Horror (Macbeth)

1

MY AUNT WAS A SOLITARY CREATURE, so the expanse of the Forres Manor suited her. It was dark and drafty, draped with so many layers of history and tradition that as soon as I stood before the great double doors, I felt suffocated. Stone lions flanked the entrance. Between cracks in the stone, ivy took hold, crawling and prying the fissures open wider. Above, the sky looked metal gray. It was difficult to picture sunlight piercing through the thick blanket of clouds to shine on Forres.

I knocked again. The sound my fist made was tiny. This door needed a giant's hand to thunder on it properly.

Silence echoed within. My aunt had stated she would be present to answer the door. What if her illness had crumpled her already?

The last time I saw Aunt Hollin, she already looked thin and pale as paper. Her bones, composed of dust, hardly held together as she took little, bird-like steps from one room to the next. She was in no shape to attend to an entire manor on her own, but she insisted. History. Tradition. It was as if those gigantic, dusty concepts held her in their massive grip and wouldn't let go. My very suggestion that she find a nice cottage in which to retire sent her into a rage. So the manor grew dustier and darker the longer my aunt attempted to stave off the inevitabilities of time.

"Aunt Hollin!" I cried, tightening my grip on my leather briefcase. The air wasn't cold, exactly, but the breeze carried with it an arctic nip that sent my free hand to my collar. "I'm here!"

A groan creaked through the underused hinges as one of the double doors swung partially inward. The rooms within were black. Floating in the darkness was a little pale face framed on one side by skeletal fingers gripping the wood.

A shiver unconnected to the cold raced through me. Aunt Hollin was even frailer than I'd seen her last. She hardly seemed human, emerging out of the darkness like that. I composed myself. I'd seen frail people before, even many dying, and nursed them back to health. But oozing sores and burning fevers didn't elicit the same visceral reaction as seeing someone I knew peering at me as if from the grave.

"Aunt Hollin," I greeted, afraid to take her hand for fear of crushing it in my own. "So good to see you. May I come in?"

The door objected loudly to being pried open further, but she shuffled to one side and let me enter.

"Why don't you strike the lights?"

Aunt Hollin's burning eyes scrutinized me. Another

shiver skittered down my back. Something was wrong here beyond her illness.

"William," she rasped, like another smaller door creaking. Her stare found my medical kit. "Dr. William Porter now."

"That's right," I affirmed. "I've been practicing for three years. Since shortly after I saw you last."

She grunted. The door behind us remained ajar. Without the streaky light pouring in from without, I doubted I could have seen anything. Why did she stay in this darkness like some creature instead of a human being whose companionship was with the living?

I tried again. "It truly is dark here, Aunt. I can hardly feel comfortable in such a situation. If you'd be so kind to—"

"Hell is murky."

My mouth fell open. "I beg your pardon."

"Heaven does not see what she does here."

I spluttered, reaching for words. "I... What on earth? Who's *she*?" My aunt had finally lost her wits, it seemed. But her wraith-like body and ominous pronouncements smacked more of demonic possession than a mere affliction of the mind. Perhaps I'd made a mistake to come at all.

No. No, I assured myself. I was a professional. Aunt Hollin had always been queer, and now she required my aid. My expertise lay chiefly in physical medicine, but I had a basic working knowledge of the structure of the brain as well, and the ways its malfunction could manifest as adverse symptoms. I looked more closely at my aunt's gaunt face. Skin stretched over pointed cheekbones. A pale mouth cut a small slash beneath a pink, blade-like nose. And her eyes were fully dilated, almost entirely black. A consequence of dwelling in that blackness, no doubt.

"Come in," she said, ignoring my question and laying a hand once more upon the doorframe.

"I must insist you draw up some light before you shut us in," I said, my voice taking on a paternal quality I hated to use with someone of my aunt's age and experience.

Her dry eyebrows ticked downward. "The light is for her. All else is dark."

Again, that creeping sensation of the supernatural crawled across my skin. I didn't care for it at all. "In that case, I think it even more important. You called for my help, and I can hardly conduct business in darkness." I hated the idea of leaving Aunt Hollin like this, but she paused for long enough that I considered it.

As my eyes began to adjust to the heavy dark, shapes rose around me, dim and monstrous as a fairy tale about man-eating giants. The huge staircase I remembered would groan like an old man and prevent me from sleep as a boy. Beyond that, an enormous table, heavy and thick, glittered with cobwebs as if set for dead royalty.

To my knowledge, Forres did not have the luxury of modern lighting, having come from an earlier, more savage age. Perhaps it wasn't more savage, I reflected, but merely earlier, since every generation liked to vilify the one before it. Therefore, every step of progress was inevitable and the men and women fading into old age were fools not to recognize it. Forres had its dignity. It had its time, but now it had sunk as inexorably toward the grave as my poor aunt.

With a scowl, she thrust her bony hand into a pocket

and produced a small matchbook. "You don't know best," she said, "but I suppose your eyes are weak."

I clamped my mouth shut to prevent a defensive response. Aunt Hollin was suffering from weakness, delusions, possibly hallucinations and lightness of the brain. The right thing was to let her say her piece. My time would come when I examined her.

When she approached a wall sconce too high for her, I insisted on taking the light from her and doing the task myself. She didn't argue, as I feared she would. We made a grim procession, walking most of the circumference of the enormous room, adding lights lights lights.

The result of our work illuminated the grisly sight. The huge rugs strewn by the entryway, the large table, were all stained with brown and rust-colored grime. Spiders made kingdoms in the high corners. Tasseled cloth covered the portraits that once stood in this hall in funerary black. The Scottish unicorn carved into the stone fireplace had been damaged. Now its eye appeared wide with horror due to a chunk missing there on its face.

It had been years since I mused upon the beauty of strangeness, but there would have been a time, perhaps five years ago, when the very weirdness of the manor would have enchanted me. Even in my terror, I thrilled to listen to that groaning staircase as a child. I chased ghosts in the wood and listened for sylphs in the air. That was before I became a practical man of science. Medicine cured the ills of the world and banished chemical demons from their strongholds in the minds of the innocent. The strange beauty of this decaying manor swept over me like a breeze, bearing me back to that earlier state of fascination, but the sensation was quickly replaced by a shudder.

The sight wasn't one of preternatural enchantment. It was one of a rapidly aging woman incapable of maintaining this property to a livable standard. She was weak and ill. If anything, this manor was like a monster, jaws agape, ready to swallow her at last.

"There," I said, retrieving my case which I had set by the door. "Much better. Now I can get a better look at you."

She peered back at me, wary as an animal.

Seeing she would not fall into easy conversation, I stated my business directly. "Is there a place where you would be most comfortable for the examination?"

"What examination?"

"Why, the one you called me here to conduct." Had she forgotten already? Poor woman. Her stare unnerved me, but that was just a symptom of her diseased mind. How could one not feel for the real woman trapped within?

"The examination is for *her*."

My brows lowered. "Who is this *she* you keep referring to?" I had heard of individuals breaking within their psyche to the degree that they only recognized themselves in pieces, to which they gave separate names and personalities. With an uncomfortable adjustment of my fingers on the leather handle of the medical kit, I considered how far outside my level of expertise this case had grown.

"The lady of the house."

"My dear aunt, you are describing yourself. As keeper of the manor, you could be considered the current lady of the house."

"She is ill," Hollin insisted. "She dwells upstairs."

I craned to follow the sweeping staircase to its murky

top. "Upstairs? Did you move upstairs? I seem to remember you had a chamber on the main floor."

"I do. She controls the manor. She dwells upstairs."

When I turned my eyes to her again, her scowling demeanor had shrunk to something less sure. The pain beneath showed through. Though her eyes still looked too black, her posture suggested real fear.

"My dear aunt," I soothed, "whoever are you talking about?"

"The lady. She will not like these lights to look upon her deeds. She requires one candle at her bedside at all times. One candle is all she needs."

"Well, I insist on sight, so these lights will remain for the duration of my stay here." As a grown man of science, I couldn't let the ghost stories of my youth haunt me. In a manor as old and storied as Forres, there were stories, of course. I used to sit in front of that very unicorn—now in a perpetual state of fright—and listen to my older brother (God rest his soul) regale us with tales of the murders and supernatural happenings around this estate. There were witches and illusions of bloody faces and all manner of thing that used to send gooseflesh prickling up my arms. It was all in good fun, until I encountered the damning effects of demon possession myself.

Maybe that was dramatic. I had no proof it was possession. A mere affliction of the mind was more likely, but no matter the depth to which I studied the anatomical workings of the body, I could not root out the heart of my mystery. Day and night my failure gnawed at me. Was it possible that Aunt Hollin and I suffered a similar affliction, yet unknown to modern science?

I hadn't been this on edge in years. It was this place,

this person, these stories of mysterious women upstairs. I didn't relish the thought of spending the night.

Mentally, I shook myself. "You can ensure that the lady has her candle as well. In the meantime, I have had a long day's travel and would like somewhere I could lay my bags."

Perhaps my aunt would be more amenable to an examination in the morning, but I had my doubts.

Needing very little, I'd packed only a few necessities for my stay at Forres. The manor resided far enough away from the nearest town as to be inconvenient for a single day's sojourn. Mental preparation had done little to steel me against the idea of laying my head down in this cursed place.

"Shall I direct you to the master's room?" Aunt Hollin asked. Some of her crispy exterior chipped away to reveal the deep-seated persona of hostess she wore underneath.

"That will do very well."

Her tiny steps could hardly have been smaller had she been a newborn fawn. I measured my gait accordingly, but doing so felt absurd. I was a giant pantomiming painfully slow motion. Luckily, my aunt didn't seem to notice, or if she did, the fact didn't perturb her. We passed the enormous groaning staircase, the unicorn fireplace, the thick table—there was a tartan runner I hadn't noticed before—and toward the back of the house. I had the uneasy sensation of being swallowed by some great creature the deeper I traversed into its halls.

We reached the edge of the meager light I'd insisted upon. Only then did Aunt Hollin turn down a hallway I knew well and produce a key from her skirts. With much clanking in the lock, she scraped open the door. Inside was a well-appointed, dusty room consisting of a four-poster bed against the far wood-paneled wall, a chest of drawers, and a stuffed chair with cream and red stripes. On the wall was a portrait of the erstwhile "master". Legends abounded of his temper and the means through which he'd acquired the property, but my aunt belonged to an older time that demanded respect of all old things, which meant never questioning it. The exception, for her, seemed to be this business of the lady upstairs. Perhaps she'd invented an authority to legitimize her staying in this crumbling relic. Under the right management, the manor could become a noble addition to the Scottish landscape again, but in its current state, the stately outside belied its terrible state within.

"Thank you, Aunt," I said, easing off my traveling coat and setting my case by the bed.

Without a word, she left me to myself. The air expanded at her departure. The shrewd madness in her gaze had left my chest tight. Madness certainly had gripped her. A pity that she did not seem keen for my help, so she could find relief and spend her remaining days in peace.

I would have to convince her of the soundness of the idea. Glancing about the room, I hoped it would not take long.

2

The night passed without monsters, although I did hear a disconcerting number of noises. Voices too, but those always beat on my mind. The subconscious presented ideas to the mind that consciousness wouldn't abide. It was God's own invention not to let others see into our thoughts in sleep. Dreams suggested the very worst of me. In them, I killed, I suffered, I watched as red blood oozed from cracks in the wainscoting.

I was extremely glad for sunrise. With the dawn came sanity and the certainty that there was no ghostly woman upstairs, only the afflicted imagination of my aunt.

Cracking open a soft-boiled egg with a spoon to spread it on toast, I smiled. "Do you ever take strolls on the heath, Aunt Hollin?"

"I'd catch a chill," she replied from where she sat across from me.

I'd avoided the massive table in the open front area, and instead opted for a small round table situated next to the kitchen. In times gone by, it might have been for servants, but it suited me just fine.

"It's chilly in this house as well," I replied. Without asking her permission, I'd searched all the drawers in my room and the adjoining ones until I found a matchbook—larger than the one she carried on her person—and proceeded to light every candle, lantern, and fireplace I could find on the ground level. All that light made for a warmer, cheerier space. The light also illumined new aspects of the manor's state of disrepair, but I still found it infinitely preferable to the bleak dimness Aunt Hollin preferred.

She harumphed. "The lady doesn't like it when I'm gone."

I set down my knife. "Now, Aunt Hollin, enough with this nonsense about a lady upstairs."

She set both of her bony hands on the table. The slate-gray light from the windows and the candle I'd set on the table glowed on the small hairs protruding from her knuckles and chin. The weather was already beginning to turn. It would be a stormy morning. My hopes of a pleasant walk were dashed with the first rumble of thunder that echoed across our breakfast table. Forres Manor may as well have been a grange from one of the leather-and-gold-bound books stacked on my chest of drawers: *Frankenstein, Dracula, The Mysteries of Udolpho…* There seemed to be a gloomy theme among the volumes. Although not supernatural in nature compared to the rest, *Oedipus Rex* had always made me uneasy, and that thin volume sat atop the rest. Add to this the ominous warnings about a lady upstairs and my patience quickly declined.

"Do not call foul what is fair!" Hollin sniffed, eyes flashing.

"I made no such judgment, and it wouldn't matter if I had, since the lady in question does not exist."

"Your father is dead."

The change in conversation, such as it was, jarred me to silence. My father, the grandchild of the man portrayed in the oil portrait in my room, was a harsh, ambitious man, now dead, it was true. I did not want to consider the circumstances. A self-inflicted wound, the examiner had said. That was probably the truth.

Aunt Hollin continued. "He will not inherit the estate."

Finally sensing her point, I interjected, "I assure you, I don't have designs on this property, Aunt Hollin."

"Designs," she scoffed. A meaningless repetition. "You will inherit it with or without your designs. The lady does not wish you to have it."

"I intend to sell this house to someone with the means

to restore it to its former glory." But something in her tone portended threat. "This woman—"

"The lady."

"Yes, the lady. If she does not appreciate my being here to help you, then I must speak with her."

I had meant to jog some recollection in my aunt's mind that perhaps this lady she referred to was a figment of her imagination. Instead, she grew even paler. Blue and red veins crossed her temples under the skin. She reminded me of a corpse, or perhaps the transparent fish one sees in textbooks.

"The lady doesn't speak to anyone. She is frightfully grand. And she sleeps."

I sighed. "She sleeps. But you said she wishes to have a light by her. Isn't that what you told me?"

"It is. She says so." At my expression, she added, "She speaks only to herself."

"Ah."

Aunt Hollin frowned, evidently understanding my train of thought, that she herself was the lady she spoke of, speaking to herself when the house was empty. "No 'ah.' Watch with me."

"When does the lady stir?"

"Hell is murky."

She'd said that before. I made a note in my mind to write down her symptoms at a convenient time. *Paranoia, repetition, delusions, possible hallucinations…*

"When the house is dark?" I guessed.

"In the wee hours," she confirmed. "Shall I tell you of another time? He won't believe us."

Thinking of herself in multiples or in royal pronouns.

"Please do explain. The more I hear of this lady and your belief in her, the more my curiosity burns to know more."

Her gaze slid past me to the window. "Six months ago, the sky went dark. By the clock, it was day, but by the light, it was night. I've never seen a thing like that before or since. Not a mere eclipse," she snapped, "nor clouds. Murky darkness. Night darkness."

I shivered. "Do you remember the day?" I asked casually, although my blood chilled unnaturally at her description. Six months ago…

"April twenty-third, I believe it was."

I blinked. Everything inside my body raged, but I attempted to keep a cool exterior. If Aunt Hollin knew to observe the signs of horror within me, she surely would have seen them: stifled breathing, trembling fingers, blurred vision, and sweat pooling under my collar. The skin of my face felt like cold putty I could pull off.

"I see."

"The lady walked that night too."

"I see."

"You're a fool to disbelieve."

I shrugged on the armor of science once more. These misgivings were mere phantoms. "I believe what I can touch and see, Aunt Hollin. If you claim the lady walks at night, I'll watch with you and confirm it. Shall I?"

Her thin shoulders relaxed. "She won't be pleased to see you, but she needs your assistance."

"While I'm here," I said, sensing an opening, "would you like me to take a look at you as well? It's not often a doctor makes house calls here. Perhaps something in your nutrition could be altered to benefit your strength."

I think she suspected my true motives, because she answered, "Perhaps tomorrow."

"I intend to leave tomorrow. Today would be better. But have it as you like, Aunt." My next bite, as I strove for nonchalance, was dry and tasteless.

Did she know about April the twenty-third? Was this her addled way of accusing me? I didn't do anything to Father. I wouldn't. That nightmare was mere coincidence.

She bustled up from the table. I could not shake the notion that she was more creature than human. The manner with which she rose from the table, swift and wary as a startled rabbit—an old, injured one, it was true—solidified the fancy. She'd always been odd and aloof, but this additionally strange behavior was the consequence of a long term shut up alone in this draughty house.

She gathered the dishes. "I will show her to you tonight. Do not put on your nightclothes. I will fetch you when the moon is out. She doesn't want the sun to know what she is doing."

I managed through strong effort not to shiver visibly. "What is the lady doing when she emerges?"

She pursed her lips as if to shush me, but no sound came out. A warning finger rose instead. "It is not for me to speak of it. When you see her, then you'll know."

Visions of her possible activities passed before my eyes like a haunted gallery. I had no shortage of cursed images to dredge forth. Again, I wondered about demons. A foolish notion. This lady existed no more than my nightmares. Why I let them prey upon my imagination, I didn't know. Watching the minutes of the night would put to rest my perturbed thoughts and allow me to get on with the real business of tending to my aunt.

3

Sleep didn't come for me that night. Aunt Hollin was due to fetch me any time, so I could watch for the ghostly lady. The more I remained in my bed, however, the more my thoughts grew muddled, waking and dreaming became one, and the portrait of the manor's old master stared directly at me with an attitude of shrewd kinship. They said he murdered for the property, both his lord and then his best friend who suspected his involvement. Clans at the time brooked no opposition to what they deemed "natural lords," which made his crime all the more heinous. It was unprovoked against a good master, solely for personal gain.

I left a candle burning by the bedside. My aunt had warned me not to don bedclothes, so I lay on top of the deep blankets of the four poster, trying and failing to summon sleep. The stone and plaster of the walls glittered in the flickering light. How different spaces looked in nighttime! How different they appeared to an owner than a tenant! I'd started to notice cracks in the plaster I intended to shore up once the property officially descended to me. One long crack looked like a monster's frown. Another spidered from the corner in a sort of burst. Was it due to excessive humidity or age or the carelessness of previous owners?

Again, my eyes returned to the portrait. Draped in the family tartan across the shoulders, the man stood straight with a look of imperious censure on his face. The expression was a dare. *This belongs to me*, it said. *Would you defy me by taking it?*

I attempted to hold his gaze, to respond, *Yes*. Forres Manor descended to me. I would do with it what I saw fit.

The eyes became searching, mocking, violent…

I looked away.

A curt knock made me inhale sharply. "Doctor Porter? It's time. Answer the door." My aunt's shrewish voice filtered through the thick wood of my chamber door.

I rolled off the covers and hooked the candlestand in the crook of my finger to have light as I answered the door. "Well, then?" I said, as I followed her swiftly retreating form back to the main room. "Has she appeared?"

She turned back to me with her finger on her lips, a clear sign to listen instead of speaking.

I bit my tongue. She had left only one dim flame alight to honor my wishes. If anything, the choice made the room the haunt of shadows. They crawled over every surface. Even if this lady did not appear—an inevitable end to this eerie vigil—my aunt might think she had by the very tenor of the room. There in the corner lurked a shadow that looked like my father, if I didn't peer at it straight on. My chest tightened with apprehension that grew moment by moment into annoyance.

Wanting to settle this matter once and for all, I didn't indulge my desire to make my ailing aunt sit down and listen to all the reasons this foolish errand defied reason. I would cite scientific articles I'd recently read on such phenomena to satisfy my curiosity. I would tell her that her mind and body were failing. I would tell her there was no woman upstairs. To think otherwise was to believe in the boogeyman.

In my haste, I had forgotten to bring my medical kit. Aunt Hollin had called me here to check up on this phantom, after all, but, as there was no ghost in the manor, I didn't call attention to my act of forgetfulness.

Instead, we waited, loosely facing the grand staircase as if the mysterious lady would descend at any moment, clad in an evening gown, ready for photographs. No sound stirred the room but the crackle of two candle flames and the sigh of wind over the moor outside. The atmosphere played tricks with my childhood memories of ghost stories. This setting was too near perfect for me, even as a man of science, not to be affected. The cobweb-strewn banister and shadowy recesses of the room, the wide-eyed stone unicorn and utter darkness at the top of the landing all suggested haunting.

Light is perceived, when it is low, by the rods surrounding the retina, I began chanting to myself, the words as much a spiritual talisman as the seal of Solomon or a rabbit's foot.

Time stretched around us. Despite my aunt's frailty, she never wavered on her feet. Instead, her burning eyes, black in a pale face, gazed steadfastly at the empty staircase. The intensity with which she watched made me feel like I had been roused from sleep to attend a séance. As if she called to the spirits above.

I disliked that notion so entirely that I began recalling chapters from my medical textbooks with even more vigor. At one point, I may have whispered the words aloud.

The shadow resembling my father grew larger, wavering with the flame's movement, as if he would start toward me.

I didn't shut my eyes, though the effort to keep them open required more strength minute by minute.

Those bloody wounds were inflicted by his own hand. The examining physician declared it the likeliest scenario. As everyone was satisfied with that tragic explanation—as much as a grieving family could be—there was no further inquiry into the circumstances of his demise. No one searched for the bloody knife, which the maid suggested she may have cleaned automatically, since there was a sink at hand. No one asked the family anything besides what had plagued him before he chose this dreadful path. Money troubles, my mother said, because that was what everyone said in moments like those. Depression, I added, being intimately acquainted with bouts of low spirits myself. Afterwards, the body was taken away, the wide, splashing pool of blood on the kitchen floor mopped up, and a funeral held. I had only been visiting, so I left as soon as the service was held. That vision in the kitchen cropped up behind my eyelids often without the actual location blocking my access to other parts of the house. Blood is many colors, you see. It is purple and pale red and brown. It glistens in pools and dots the walls. It congeals in knife wounds. It sometimes happens, the examining physician said, that suicide victims can stab themselves more than once. I counted nine times. It sometimes happens.

My aunt twisted to glare at me.

My heart pummeled like a jackrabbit against my ribs in response.

"You've angered her," she declared in a fierce undertone.

"What have I done?" I responded, too sharply. Having no outlet for my tension made me unintentionally harsh.

"Your desire for the manor, maybe. I don't know, but she isn't walking tonight."

I glanced up the stairs to the inky blackness at the top. "Are you certain?"

"Not tonight."

That meant we'd have to copy this charade once again tomorrow. The idea brought restless heaviness to my bones. "Aunt Hollin," I sighed, "this lady of yours will not walk tomorrow either. She is a phantasm born of your own isolation in this place. Don't you see what it has done to your mind?"

A sting across my cheek ricocheted through my limbs. She had slapped me. "Don't speak dishonorably of the lady! I swear on my bones that she walks, and you are here as witness!"

I hadn't witnessed anything, but, as that was painfully evident, I did not bother to point it out.

"She speaks of things she shouldn't." This time, her voice grew so small I was forced to lean forward to catch the words. The proximity, after being slapped, felt foolish. I didn't want to be dressed down again in the name of some made-up apparition. "You'll hear them when she walks. You will be a witness."

I straightened again. "Good night, Aunt." No more words lived in me. Irrational anger, irrational fear, irrationality of all kinds had been given free reign like the spirits of Pandemonium, and I would have no more of them tonight.

Stalking back to my bedroom with the candle held before me, now almost melted down, I caught a glimpse of red. Blood? The knife? It seemed to hover before me, as solid as I'd seen it in my room after the body was taken away. It was a false creation of the brain, nothing more, but the vision persisted, following me to my chamber door. I stared at it.

The lens focuses light through the vitreus humor and onto the retina...

I reached out for the hilt. Gouts of blood spotted it, just like they had then. There were many logical reasons why such a thing could be found in any part of the house. My family owned horses and chickens, among other farm animals. Daggers were a household staple.

My fingers met steel.

It was the door handle.

4

The next day arrived groggily. I'd been forced to consume a sedative in order to get any rest the night before, and I felt the worse for wear.

By the time Aunt Hollin brought me a breakfast of toast and stewed tomatoes, I was in no mood to prevaricate. A burn mark on the table beneath my plate suggested it might have begun in the shape of a crest. I should have that restored. Everywhere there was dereliction and decay that I needed to put right. I doubted I could abide staying another day, but each instant provided more proof that this manor would collapse without me.

I stabbed a tomato and waved it toward my aunt. Her eyes grew smaller, shrewish, with suspicion, but I couldn't hide my mood. Nor would I, after last night's escapade. "I leave today, Aunt. Please let me examine you before I go, so this trip can amount to more than wasted time."

"You did not journey down to see me. Of that I am well aware," she huffed.

"I did. I did, Aunt Hollin, because I care about your health and wellbeing, which is obviously suffering under great strain in this house."

"Poppycock."

I slammed the butt on my fork on the counter, creating a new mark I would need to sand smooth again. "It is true whether you choose to believe it or not. I saw a person in need and came to offer assistance. I am not here for phantoms or any other such nonsense. Let me examine you."

"No."

My chest tightened dangerously. I squeezed the fork before setting it down on the plate. *I may have to use restraints.* The thought chagrined me. "You are incapable of surviving here on your own."

"Really, William! What a thing to say to your elders!"

"I will repeat it until I am heard. You need help."

"I need to be listened to."

"I am listening!" I shouted, rising.

My aunt looked tiny, no bigger than a terrier, still seated below me at the table. "I will not consent to some foolish examination when larger issues and greater personages are at stake. You would do well to prioritize, nephew." Now her twiggy bones seemed wrought of steel. She would never die. She would outlive me. Too much fire and iron lived in her veins.

I wouldn't stand for it, not when the table needed planing and re-branding, and cobwebs waved like ghosts between posts in the banister. This was the house of a lord, not a delusional old woman.

She continued. "The lady takes her lineage directly

from the McIshbel clan. That's something to be treated with respect."

"McIshbel murdered his lord and best friend."

"Shh shh!" She laid a skinny finger to her lips.

"I will not be silent," I cried, refusing to sit. "He was an evil tyrant. In fact, I want his portrait removed from my room."

She merely gave a derisive noise. My aunt was probably too weak to lift such a heavy object as the gilt-framed portrait anyway.

My gaze drifted to the main room, with its black-draped gallery of McIshbel faces.

My mother was McIshbel, last of her clan, but she'd married an Englishman named Porter. The decision was not a popular one among her few remaining relatives at the time. Technically, that made me the last of the McIshbel clan, after Aunt Hollin passed away, although I didn't admit to the name.

The entire history of McIshbels was soaked in blood, from its earliest memory to the terrible scene six months ago. Now, my aunt stood between me and the only good things I had to my name: my medical education and practice, and my inheriting the manor.

"You think me a fool," she said, rising too. Her eyes fell on my uneaten plate of food. I placed a possessive hand on its edge. "Watch with me one more night to confirm I am not mad. It is the lady who needs your assistance. It is she who suffers!"

I drew in a deep inhalation through my nose, striving for peace. "If this figure does not appear by midnight, I will leave immediately." I held up a hand. "I am fully aware of how dark the road becomes after nightfall. I'm prepared to brave it rather than stay on a fool's errand any longer than is necessary."

The thin wrinkled in her forehead deepened. "She's not on anyone's timetable." But she seemed to emanate some relief that I had agreed to watch with her once again.

My blood chilled at my own declaration. I had no desire to trundle out into the darkness of the moors. The cloudy skies of late wouldn't even admit of moonlight to guide the way. Neither did I want to encounter some phantom woman floating through the manor like a disease.

One or the other, however, would happen tonight.

5

I, like many others, am afflicted with sleepwalking. At least I was informed of that fact in my youth. I tell you this to assure you that I was not sleepwalking that night, although my perception blurred slightly under the burden of the late hour and scant light. To prove my sincerity in this matter, I will relay the circumstances exactly as they occurred, assisted by notations I made in my medical notebook.

That night, I remembered to bring my medical kit, along with the stub of a pen and a few pages on which to write notes. My reasoning was that I could continue to document Aunt Hollin's evident ailments of the mind, so I could bring an accurate report back to someone I knew who specialized in mental afflictions more than I did. Physical medicine was my area of expertise. The mental sciences were a mere hobby.

"We have stayed awake for two nights, and this person

has not made an appearance," I whispered. The shot of brandy I'd taken to calm my nerves seemed only to make me more irritable.

Aunt Hollin did not acknowledge me. Instead, she pointed a skeletal finger to the blind landing at the top of the stairs. It was no longer inky black, but dark like a depth of sea. The forcible comparison made me focus on my breathing, in and out. I stood in an ordinary pocket of air, so there was no reason for my breathing to be labored. The faint transition from black to deepest blue unnerved me, however. That meant that either the clouds had parted outside for the first time in days, which was my prime suspicion, or an additional light had been lit upstairs.

My aunt had said something that first day about how the lady required light by her side. How did she keep it lit unless she crept upstairs at moments when I didn't watch her? That would mean the action was most likely done in the deadest part of night. I didn't find the thought of her crawling up those stairs alone in the darkness at all agreeable. The very notion made Aunt Hollin seem monstrous.

I inhaled and exhaled slowly once more.

"There," she said.

And there was something there. A dim figure at the top of the stairs, descending. Thick night, like the smoke of hell, prevented me from seeing clearly. At first, I thought it was a man, but then I recognized it as a strong woman, dressed in a nightgown, finger hooked around the loop in a candlestand. Her features grew clearer with every step she took. Dark, unbound hair fell wildly around her shoulders and white face. Her eyes were open, but not fixed on either of us, who silently watched her approach. She had the expression of someone searching their own mind.

Only when she reached the final stair did I see the blood. Blood can be black as well. The low light had rendered everything in monochrome, but now that she stood mere steps away, I saw the truth. Blood coated her hands, running down her forearms when she lifted the candle. A smudge of red graced her cheek as if she'd pushed hair away from her face and accidentally transferred the substance there.

Too late I remembered my little notebook. I moved slowly, like a small creature in the sights of a predator, to retrieve it.

Aunt Hollin laid a feather-light hand on my arm. "She doesn't see us," she breathed.

"How can that be?" I stared, transfixed, at the woman, who looked less like a ghost and more like a banshee ready to scream. My heart seized, waiting for the dreadful noise.

"Her eyes are open, but their sense is shut."

No more candle flickered in her grip. Instead, she seemed to glow from within. Only the creeping flow of blood down her arms, dripping from her fingers, dimmed the light.

Sleepwalking, I jotted. *A great perturbation of nature. Something preys on her mind.*

The lady's head swiveled slowly from side to side, gaze keen but unseeing. Her attention never once lighted on us. If it had, I was afraid I'd have gone mad. Her eyes were too piercing, as if they could see through walls, through obstacles, and push through. The dark room where we stood was too inconsequential.

Suddenly, her focus shifted to something more immediate—her blood-sheathed hands. "Here's a spot," she muttered, rubbing at her drenched palm.

It was more than a spot. The flow of blood would have reddened all the Mediterranean before the waters could have cleansed her fingers.

Blood, I wrote. *Calls a torrent a mere spot.*

"Damn spot!" she cried, flicking her hands now. Droplets flew across the floor and speckled my front, but I didn't dare to move. The minute gestures of my fingers as I wrote down her words were my only exception.

Aunt Hollin gazed almost worshipfully. Her being was lost in this spaceless rent in time. We were all three suspended. I was no longer Dr. Porter who had consumed fried potatoes and stew for lunch, nor was I Dr. Porter who fell off a horse when he was six and laid in bed for two weeks after. I was not the Dr. Porter who had chosen this blue shirt in the morning. I was transmogrified into someone else who only touched *that* Dr. Porter's life at intervals. My writing was like the automatic writing of mediums, swift and messy to record every grain of an otherworldly message.

The bottom of the lady's white nightgown dragged with red blood. It was not hers, yet it belonged to her. I knew well there were two kinds of belonging.

"It's time to do it," she whispered. Then, louder, "Why are you afraid? A doctor, and afraid? What have we to fear?"

My hand moved. My heart frosted over.

"Who would have thought the old man to have had so much blood in him?"

I wrote it even though I saw my death in the cramped characters.

"Do you mark that?" Aunt Hollin's mouth barely moved.

I didn't answer.

The lady moved more frantically, wiping her hands on her skirts and only managing to soil them. "What? Fie!" she cried. A puddle was forming at her feet. "Will these hands never be clean?" She scrubbed at them, the image growing more horrible. Nothing she attempted stemmed the flow that dripped from her heart. "Ack! Everything smells of blood! No spice or salve will sweeten it."

I remembered a time I was myself in Dr. Porter's body. There were spices in little jars.

"The caretaker of the manor. Where is she now?" The lady's eyes did not alight on my aunt, but the reference to the frail person beside me brought me halfway out of my stupor. My next deep breath made me dizzy.

Where is she now? The soft tap of the dot below the question mark echoed throughout the room. All my other writing hadn't sounded so loud.

That movement, however, drew the ghost's attention to my face. The hair on my neck, my arms, and everywhere, stood rigid. The lady's glow expanded to take me in.

"Wash your hands, put on your nightgown, and don't look so pale," she instructed, blood dripping from her fingernails. She said it with no small amount of kinship, as if she understood my challenges of late, yet was above them. My life was a path that she had trod long ago. "I tell you again, he cannot rise from the grave." She blinked, strange in her presence and absence at once. The dark eyes consumed me. "Go to bed. Come, give me your hand. What's done cannot be undone."

I gazed at her alarming hand, now outstretched to me.

One of my hands held the candle, the other free to take hers. She knew what I had done, knew and did not condemn except to show her own wretchedness. Company in misery.

I took her hand. Blood already welled on my skin. Perhaps it had been mine on her to begin with, rather than hers on mine. The lady led me back through the darkened great room to my bed chamber. With her by my side, my mind flamed with history, with violence, with ease. I was alive in this sort of death. When we reached my room, she deposited me without a word and closed the door.

6

The view outside the windows next day was radiant. The thick blanket of grey clouds had parted to reveal green slopes and trees that grew much closer to the manor than I had reckoned in the earlier fog. The kitchen smelled oddly metallic. Tomatoes or spinach could have such an effect on the mind. In good spirits, I wandered slowly to inspect the space.

When my aunt didn't emerge from whatever hiding place she stowed herself, I called her name. No snappish answer replied.

Drawing my brows together, I searched beyond the kitchen. No lights illuminated the dilapidated great room save the morning sun streaming through the windows. Even more flaws and eyesores presented themselves in the rich light. There was a tear in the Persian rug before the mantel. A lump of black fabric lay on the ground beneath a stately portrait of Lady McIshbel. She had long, unbound hair around a pale face. Plans for painters and carpenters occupied my thoughts so forcefully that by the time I investigated the staircase, I was thinking not of the dust and stains there, but of a new gravel drive that could support horses and motorists to assist at the house. I would plant trees to shield the house from unwanted visitors, and I'd install a gate I could monitor freely. Only those interested in assisting with my project of returning Forres Manor to its former glory would gain admittance.

"Aunt Hollin!" I shouted at the base of the stairs.

She was a stubborn woman, too stubborn to have let me apply my medical knowledge in diagnosing her. I suspected she had deterioration of the bones and paranoid delusions, a dreadful combination. Why wouldn't she allow me to tend to her? Instead, she had to be so damn willful.

"Aunt Hollin!"

After a thorough search of the main floor and a cursory look outside, I determined my aunt not on the premises at all unless she had gone upstairs. Someone had had to light the lady's candle, after all.

The thought of crossing onto the first stair was unpleasant. After my aunt's warnings, the area had become a sort of forbidden fantasyland, where diseases and spirits lurked. Summoning my courage with the remonstrating idea that I was a man, not a child, I ascended the steps. The air grew sharper, as it had in the kitchen, and, as it did, so too did my senses.

This moment bore an uncomfortable similarity to another time, not long back, when I had searched for someone in vain, only to discover them where I did not expect.

The top of the landing held no monsters, only furniture

covered by dusty white sheets along a wide hallway peppered with doors. One of them was ajar. Was that the lady's room? I was loathe to disturb her, especially in the daylight when she had no business to be moving about.

I considered calling out again, but the sound died in my throat.

Placing my palm upon the door handle, I pushed to see inside. It was white and red, with a figure at the center upon the bed. I approached.

It was Aunt Hollin. Her face was pale, as it always was, and red too. But blood is many colors. It was red on the white sheets and brown on the ground. There was so much of it that the places where it pooled at her chest and neck were a deep purple. In her hair it looked sticky and pink.

I'm not sure if I was surprised to find her there. She was always going to be there. What was done was done. I blew out the candle still burning low at her bedside. Grief at her condition and elation at my turn of fortune melded until all I experienced was a profound contemplation.

Yes, I would create a new drive. I would plant new trees. I would have a portrait done to add to the existing gallery in the hall. I would dress in my best family tartan or get an even better one to wear for special occasions.

In my roving to find my aunt—of course I should have known where she was—I noticed half a rhubarb pie in the ice box. It offended my manners to consider eating dessert for breakfast, but it was such a lovely day that the wind itself seemed to urge me to overstep the boundary.

for anne hathaway

. . .

Elegiac poetry

second best

WHAT WAS FIRST?

I sang for him and he called my song
The food of love.
Old, at twenty-six, I sucked the honey
Of his music vows,
Glad of brilliant company. His mind to me
Theatrical—it paragoned description and wild fame.

His words mellifluous and melancholy,
Sharp, witty, they crash like steel
With a grin and a sidelong eye—
Little stones cracked open that were gems
In the light, like heirlooms
Worn wrapped around the neck.
He chased words
Up and down the river

Carly Stevens

>Up and down the wind
>Between our houses
>Between our breath.

Tomorrow was Saint Valentine's day.
We had the motive and the cue for passion,
So I let him in, I let him out.

Never doubt I love, said he.
And I believed him.

At last our lives had rhythm past the scandal.
Our marriage came and sanded rough-edged minds.
He held Susanna tightly in his arms,
Then later taught a bit at Henley Street,
One eye on London and one on me,
Until the twins were born and he left.

Was it worth it, after all?
Alone, I watched my only son
Fade, quite, quite down.

The man, returning, sad,
Replaced my baby with a building.
Sparkling words in London all sapped at home.
His New Place smelled of dark women
And queens and foreign hands.

I sang for him when he returned at last
But soon he sickened.
Old, at fifty-two, he faded, faded,
Music with a dying fall,

For Anne Hathaway

Finally tiresome company. His mind to me
Opposed—it dreamed of others.

Youths and characters, his sons-in-law,
All held their place but me.
Death took him on his birthday in the second-best bed—
My only parting gift.

Hamlet was a masterpiece, they say.
But I say no. My Hamnet spoke and swam and scraped his hands,
And gave him cause him to speak
Words, words, and still more words!

I hear he played Hamlet's father.

christmas in paris

. . .

Vintage Christmas (Hamlet)

I HUDDLED CLOSER under the festooned white tent. Lines of them mushroomed along the Rue St. Honoré, a fairyland of rich scents and sparkling baubles. At 4:30, the sun was already sinking, drowning us in shadows.

"Will you choose already?" Julien prompted, clutching his wassail in gloved hands.

Henri didn't look up from the earrings he'd been admiring for far too long.

Julien set down his cup on the vendor's table and picked up one set. Delicate bronze chains connected two variously sized dark gems—smaller at the top and larger hanging below. "Jewels," he said. He demonstrated the next pair. A slim rectangle of diamonds attached to the ear while an oval pearl dangled beneath. "More jewels."

"Neither one speaks of Josephine," Henri mused.

Julien heaved a sigh.

"She has an emerald soul."

I hummed my agreement, simply to prevent Julien's retort. In an odd way, I understood his comparison.

Josephine was certainly more akin to dark green than white or pink, but she included many colors. I would have chosen the pearls for her, but I had little money to spend until I returned to Kronborg after the term ended and Father provided me some.

"Oh!" On the table lay a mother-of-pearl comb, just the sort Ophelia liked. "How much?" I asked the vendor, a shrewd-eyed man with a perpetual smile and fiercely parted hair. His smile was reminiscent of a villain, but he tempered the impression by wearing a red felt scarf in honor of the holiday.

We exchanged *francs* and I pocketed my treasure.

"See?" Julien punched Henri lightly in the arm. "Laertes knows how to choose and go." He scooped up his wassail and we set out again.

The nipping air stung our faces. Shoppers chatted around us, holding luxurious coats closer and taking care while walking over spots dotted with snow. Above us, in the trees, electric lights bloomed. The sight brought thickness to my throat.

When I was a child, Father would read from Andrew Lang's fairy books. Looking back, I doubt he did it very often, but I remember one Christmas sitting cross-legged with Hamlet before a tinsel-strewn tree, Father holding the Blue Fairy Book as he sat on a stool. The story was "Prince Darling", cursed to become a series of creatures until he learned to do good, as his father the king wished.

At Hamlet's request, we sipped hot chocolate as we listened. The cook added a touch of black cherry juice to each and topped the drinks with whipped cream. It was unimaginably decadent, as if we had joined a fairy tale ourselves and were moments away either from happily ever after or a shattering occurrence that would send us on a death-defying adventure.

Father's robustious voice tripped along, lingering on the drama of each moment. Each of the prince's animal transformation sent us into fits. Naturally, we both thought of Hamlet.

I flapped my knees with excitement at the part when the prince (then a dog) finds a fine meal but is warned that all food from the palace of pleasure is poisoned, and that he mustn't eat it. He transforms into a silky white dove immediately afterward and flies away.

These lights for Christmas-tide made me think of doves and magic and enchanted palaces of pleasure.

Along the cold waves of darkening air wafted the scent of roasting chestnuts. We picked some up on the way back to the Battlements. There had been no need to take out our bicycles, since the nearest Christmas market was a mere five-minute stroll from Luc's shop.

Snow clung to the metal diamonds of the fire escape, gilding it white. We clomped upstairs all together, jostling, letting the freedom of the cold and snow and impending holiday from the Sorbonne fill our veins with peppermint excitement.

We fell inside. Henri laughed, Julien cursed and reached for the skull on the mantel, and I scrambled over the two of them to get inside, toeing off my boots as I went. Our flat was too cramped to let water splash over the books and wall sketches.

"Welcome home!" crooned a sultry feminine voice. Josephine stood in the center of the main room before the piano, arms upraised in dramatic presentation. A sleeveless silver sheath shimmered in the candlelight, cutting a sharp line just above her breasts. Over that was draped a sort of dress or skirt. It was black velvet, a play on suspenders crisscrossing over the sheath and ending in a skirt longer in the back than the front. On her head was a pointed party hat.

Henri beamed. *"Mon coeur!"* He took one of her hands. "What a wonderful surprise."

"A surprise that I would be here?" she teased.

"You said you were sick," I chimed in. "We missed you at the market."

"I had no choice but to leave you boys alone to buy me gifts." She caressed the line of Henri's jaw.

His eyes shone with her attention.

"I thought you might return later," she continued, her darkly colored mouth transforming to a pout. The look reminded me of Danish girls, but on Josephine the look was surprisingly becoming. I understood why Henri blushed and encircled her waist to draw her closer. "I was still decorating."

I glanced around the room. Josephine had dominated our attention, but now that I observed the space around her, I saw she'd been busy. Red and green paper chains looped over the bookcase and across the top of the piano. Papercraft candles had been pasted to the window. A few shining ornaments had been stuffed in corners. Cuttings of pine scented the room, but now lay strewn and prickly in our best armchair.

Julien chuckled. "No place for anything now."

"I think it's marvelous," said Henri, kissing her.

I awkwardly scooped up the pine boughs. A few needles came off on my jacket sleeve. "Where did you want to put these?"

"Oh, anywhere," Josephine answered breezily.

There was a little space on the mantel, so I laid them across and set the skull atop the branches. The leering head tilted, but the overall effect was surprisingly festive.

"Charming," she declared.

I gave a half-smile.

"Shall we have a lark?" she asked.

"Yes, please. Anything to warm up," said Julien, taking up very much space as he bustled past to his room, tossing his paper cup in the bin as he went.

I followed suit, not bothering to hang my coat and scarf, but throwing them unceremoniously on the bedclothes. A little adjusting of my hair and I emerged as Julien did, sans jacket, his flat cap free of the melted snow that had begun pooling near the brim.

Henri was already seated at the piano, wearing a paper hat like Josephine's.

Julien groaned, but he was smiling. "You look like an idiot. Don't tell us you have—"

But Josephine anticipated him, producing stiff paper cut like a something for a giant's paper doll.

"I want the green one!" Julien and I cried at once. The options were deep green or orange. I didn't want to look the dunce.

My reach was longer, but only just. I cast Josephine a fractional look of apology as I snatched the uneven green triangle from her hand.

Julien cursed, pinching the rusty monstrosity between his big fingers.

She grinned evilly, bending the paper in his hand to form the cone shape. "You see, it goes just like that."

"Fuck." He inserted the paper tags into their slits.

"Now, put the hat to its right use," she said, lifting it. Julien's arm weighed it down, since he still gripped one edge, but she managed to crest the brim of his cap with this new feature and make him release the edge so she could settle it fully.

Henri and I burst out laughing.

Josephine tapped him on his large nose. "Now there's a man who could quote the poetry of Aeschylus."

His skin mottled with red, but amusement tinged the edges of his murderous stare.

Josephine's gaze slid to me, like a spotlight in a play, just as Henri began playing chords. I understood her immediately and placed my own party hat on my head.

We all looked absurd and very happy.

The chords transformed into "In a Merry Mood". Julien got the absinthe, muttering something about needing the whole bottle. I brought down glass cups. The song became "Swingin' Them Jingle Bells." Candles were lit, half-zozzled caroling ensued, and new snow swirled in the windows.

By the time we launched into a rendition of "Bring a Torch, Jeannette, Isabella" I was wearing the paper chain around my neck as a boa, with one end dangling over Henri's shoulder, I was standing so close. It struck me with force that these three were my firelight—that yellow-orange rectangle in paintings that signaled a door was open, and the door led to home and warmth and love. Bread was baking and stories flowed from one generation to the next. It didn't matter if you returned after a long absence; that firelight would welcome you home.

I smiled to myself.

"Oh!" Josephine touched my shoulder. "I'm not a

snoop, but I spied your name on a bit of mail in the hall," she whispered. I shivered at the words in my ear, then quickly shook off the sensation. Self-awareness made the night shed some of its magic.

Henri finished the song with gusto. Julien sighed, finishing his glass of absinthe in a gulp.

"From Ophelia, maybe?" Henri guessed.

"I don't know from what other part of the world I would be greeted," I agreed.

I tottered to the hall where Luc slipped our mail under the door. Sure enough, an envelope bore my name. But it wasn't my sister's handwriting. Flipping the letter over, I found the Danish royal seal.

My heart jumped. Hamlet? Hopefully all was well in Kronborg. The prince was prone to fits of sentiment, but didn't often reach out to me unless there was news to convey. We saw each other every few months at the castle already.

I ripped open the letter.

Dear Laertes,

I am currently confined to my room after eating too much gingerbread. I do not encourage comment or criticism, written or thought, for this decision. Naturally, I brought more gingerbread with me, because I cannot be reasoned with. You know this.

Perhaps I am melancholy or giddy tonight. Truly, I do not know why your sorry face should be the first in my thoughts. I know you are a gentleman and would never let the hoi polloi know my scruples. I may speak freely. Maybe that is my impetus for penning this letter to you.

The season of advent reminds me of past and future,

as it is intended, but the contrast turns my thoughts into a violence of either grief or joy. Several joyful memories involve you. (Do you ever try to trace your own happiness back to a source? It's a futile exercise. Played out, you will wind up in bed, a perfectly noble grown gentleman, after having eaten far too much gingerbread at once.)

Memory one: We were thirteen, I think (wretched age), and saw The Pirates of Penzance. We agreed to be pirates together once we were men. The profession seemed to involve nothing but antics, lovely girls, and the use of revolvers.

Memory two: Again, no hoi polloi. We were fifteen and you lost all our money in a bet with the servants. You took Fortune's buffets and rewards with equal thanks, uncomplaining. We were smoking. You lied on my behalf. Unseemly for the prince to dally so, but you understood a man's need to explore while his blood is up.

I fear I will regret this letter in the morning, so I will simply post it and go to sleep. A friendly impulse toward a fellow man is never amiss, don't you think? Mr. Dickens' Christmas ghosts all seem to agree.

God, this letter is lousy with sentimentality. The only cure is more exploration, and gingerbread.

Happy Christmas,

Hamlet

I stared at the letter, chewing the inside of my lip. It wasn't like Hamlet to reach out to me in this way. He knew he'd hate himself, but I blessed his stomachache for putting him in such an uncanny mood. Sometimes I wasn't sure if Hamlet and I were even friends. Things had become strained the past few years. We'd grown apart. Every time I saw him felt like a struggle. Fencing had become an embodiment of my desire to match him or find that childhood friendship again. My thoughts were in a tangle.

"Is it Ophelia?" cried Julien from the other room.

I cleared my throat. "No. Lord Hamlet sends a happy Christmas."

"Prince Hamlet?" Josephine asked, obviously intrigued.

I stuffed the letter back in its envelope and stuck it in my pocket as I reemerged. "Yes, just happy Christmas."

"I'm jealous," she said.

I realized I still had the paper chain round my neck. I transferred it to Henri. "Don't be."

Julien raised his eyebrows at me, a quick acknowledgment of the bits he knew of my fraught friendship with Hamlet. I gave him a small smile. It was all right. My thoughts wouldn't spiral into darkness tonight.

Tonight, no spirit dared stir abroad. No black mood would suck me down beneath this sparkling room. Merry, charming things only.

Henri played "Silent Night" while we sang along, more somber now, but no less happy. We swayed and declared a toast to the new year and to us.

also by carly stevens

Tanyuin Academy series (YA fantasy)

Firian Rising

Into the Unreal

Kingdoms on Fire

Tanyuin Academy Stories (short story collection)

Literary retellings

Laertes: A Hamlet Retelling

The Hamlet Reader (compilation of *Hamlet* research)

Cozy fantasy

Power to Charm: Cozy Stories About a Witch, a Cottage, and Unexpected Friends

———

Find more about Carly Stevens' work, including bonus stories, at
https://carly-stevens.com

about the author

Carly Stevens is a multi-genre author who writes dark and immersive books about finding hope against the odds —sometimes fantasy, sometimes dark academia, but always with a hint of magic.

To find out more about upcoming projects, check out her website: https://carly-stevens.com

Be the first to get notified about new projects when you sign up for her author newsletter!

@carlystevensbooks

www.ingramcontent.com/pod-product-compliance
Lightning Source LLC
LaVergne TN
LVHW011048100526
838202LV00078B/3917